FIFTEEN SHEKELS OF SILVER

A Divine Love Story

TERRY R. BARNWELL

Dedication

I wish to dedicate this book to my beloved family:

Sharon, Brent, Eric, Chelsea, Evan, & Amber

PS: I'm proud of you

Acknowledgements

First and foremost I must give thanks to my Lord and Savior Jesus Christ for setting me free from sin's cruel bonds. To Him, I owe all glory for everything good in my life. I give thanks and praise to my heavenly Father and The Blessed Holy Spirit for guiding me and calling me to write this book. If there is anything which touches your soul you can thank God for it. If there is anything you find as an error, you may blame me.

My family has given me unwavering support in the long duration of this project. Thank you for listening and for reading and re-reading the manuscript, while giving me good loving advice.

Countless friends have also read the manuscript, giving me feedback and encouragement throughout the journey. I thank you with all my heart!

Special thanks to my sons, Eric, & Evan for all your assistance in editing and grammar. I couldn't have done this without you. Thank you to Brent for all the hours spent on the Museum Page and other ministry projects. You men amaze me with your brilliance. It must have come from your mother.

To my extended family, I love you with all my heart. Thank you for the thousands of prayers you have prayed for me. Thank you for supporting me and challenging me to always grow in Christ.

To the church families we have cared for over the years, allow me to say that you have blessed me far more than I could ever have returned. Thank you for sharing in this ministry and taking the journey with us.

To Sharon, my wife, and best friend, I am forever grateful that God brought you into my life. You have stood beside me with unwavering love. Through many times, when I, like Gomer, didn't deserve to be loved, you never gave up on me. You are God's gift to me! Thanks honey, for everything.

Cover Art:

I am forever grateful to Mr. Jordan Holt for his professional and extensive work on the cover art. For many years, Gomer had been a figure only in my mind. Through Jordan's skill and brilliant imagination, she has come to life in vivid illustration.

The chains which hold her arms represent every captive of sin, desiring, and desperately seeking FREEDOM, through the grace of God.

Scriptural Source

Note: All scriptural references are personal translations of the author, except for those used within the story, they are KJV.

To the Reader; Before You Start...

You are about to embark upon a journey. As you travel throughout this story, sometimes you may encounter yourself, sometimes the devil, but most importantly, may you find God and His love.

This story has been in my heart for many years, tucked away in the deep recesses of my soul. But now as you turn the pages and read line by line, the story will also become your own. Take the liberty to see the characters as they appear in your mind. Allow your own imagination to paint each scene with colorful vibrancy.

While this story is fiction, it is also laced with historical places and persons. However, the intent was never to create an exact record of historical events. The purpose is to introduce the reader to biblical people, places, and customs from the story's setting.

Most importantly, as you read, please know, that you have been prayed over. I have asked God to allow this book to bless you, encourage you, and bring you to a repentant heart if you do not know Jesus Christ as your personal Lord and Savior.

I am honored to have you as one of my readers. Thank you!

Chapter 1

A Parchment Scroll Is Found

"Listen to the Word of the LORD, you Children of Israel: for the LORD has something against those who dwell in the land. There is no truth, or mercy, nor is there any knowledge of God among you."

Hosea 4:1

If he had lived a thousand years I suppose he would never have forgotten the feeling of listening to his dear Abba cry on that fateful night. Mishi knew his Abba was a strong man, invincible, and rarely showed such emotion as this. He laid still and silent not betraying the fact that he was still awake and listening to the deep conversation between Jezreel, his Abba, and Anna, his momma.

As Mishi laid there a cool eastern Jerusalem wind flowed over his face. It licked at his own tears, tightening his olive skin as it dried them. He could not understand why his heart ached so, or why it felt so heavy. All he knew was this night was different from all the rest, and as hard as he tried to understand, it was one of those moments a child can never fully grasp until they reach adulthood. For now, all he knew was his Abba was weeping and heavy hearted, and because of this Mishi wept also.

He looked up into the night sky above him and gazed at the stars illuminating the darkness. On most nights their brilliant light would fill his heart with joy, but tonight, they did little to comfort him. Normally sleeping out on the roof was most exciting, but tonight it was as though the darkness itself invaded his soul.

Mishi listened carefully as Jezreel whispered to Anna in low tones. His words were laced with anger, fear and sorrow. The wind that found its way through the lattice surrounding the courtyard of the roof carried all the tension over to Mishi; it pierced his deepest emotions like a sharp two edged sword.

Mishi's mind wandered back to earlier in the day, a day which had begun well. It was the third day of the week, which for Mishi always meant following his momma to the community oven to bake their bread. While the dough bakes, women laugh and converse together, children play, and the current happenings of the city are passed from one to another.

They had not been there long when the festive atmosphere was suddenly broken. A neighbor, Shekina, had come to fetch Anna. Shekina was an elderly woman with the Wisdom of Solomon. Often it was she who resolved arguments or quarrels in the community peacefully. "Anna," she said, attempting to catch her breath from the hurried trip to retrieve them. She sat down on the wall surrounding the clay ovens while

Mishi's momma quickly put down her basket and turned to face her.

"Three men have come to your home inquiring of your husband," said Shekina breathlessly, "they are of the priesthood from the Temple, and say they must speak to Jezreel at once!"

Even Mishi at such a young age knew that a visit from a priest was enough to set the whole community on edge. For many years there had been a separation from the priesthood and the common people. This separation was seen as a holy commitment by the priests who demanded rare interaction with anyone outside their communal brotherhood.

Mishi watched as Anna and Shekina conversed in tones that were somber and thoughtful. Then just as suddenly as Shekina's arrival, Anna and Mishi were now racing down the dusty cobblestone path leading back to their home. "What about the bread?" he asked, but Anna did not hear him. Her face was shadowed with deep thoughts and deeper questions, so he did not ask again. Finally, after a long silence, she said; "Shekina will bring the bread; it will allow her time to rest while she waits." Anna's voice was tense, gasping out words between labored breaths.

Suddenly Anna stopped, she looked down at Mishi; "I need you to go to the gate of the city and bring your father. Tell him that priestly men have come asking for him. I shall wait for you both at home." He had never seen his momma like this before! As he looked up into her eyes he could see the unanswered questions burning deep within them, "*what did these priests want with her husband, and* what was so important to bring them out into the community where they rarely came?"

After walking a short distance more, at last they reached the place where the path split. One part led up to the cluster of homes where they lived overlooking the narrow waters of the Makhtesh, and the other path led to the gate of the city where Mishi knew his Abba could be found. Anna passionately laid her hand on Mishi's shoulder, "Mishi, you must hurry now, do not delay" and as she kissed his forehead she bid him "Shalom." She turned and was gone up the path and vanished from his sight.

Mishi plunged into the rabbit warren of the city streets. Running headlong, he did not stop at the many calls of merchants, though for a young boy the smells of bread and meats baking in the roadside stands caused his mouth to water. Occasionally he would hear one of the merchants call out "fresh cheeses for sale," for along this Tyropoeon Valley there were many guilds of cheese makers.

He could soon tell that he was getting closer to the Valley Gate, for the hoards of people became almost impassable. Like tall towers they flowed around him with their cloaks and garments flapping against his face. This intense crush of people near the Valley Gate always frightened him, and now he fought back tears as he pressed through the endless sea of giants. When he came to *Millo*, his paced slowed as his search began. His Abba, he knew, could be near.

The Valley Gate served as the passageway from the City of David to the newly built annex constructed by King Hezekiah. Men came here for many reasons: business, news, and often just idle meandering. But for Jezreel it was the place of proclamation. While most days he could have been found out in the fields tending their flocks and pasturing the vineyards, on other days like this one, he came here to proclaim the ways of righteous living. If Mishi knew anything at all about his dear Abba, he knew Jezreel burned with passion to speak the cause of holiness to anyone who would listen. It was as though his Abba's blood boiled to avenge evil and turn hearts toward God.

It wasn't long until Mishi heard Jezreel's voice thundering, and authoritative, shouting out above all the commotion surrounding him;

"Turn to God with all your hearts or He will break the bow of Israel!"

Once Mishi found him in his vision he walked over and sought out a place among the few who were listening. He stood there for a brief moment as one of the assembly. Jezreel, from his lofty place upon a stone which had been cast aside by some builder, continued his discourse. Mishi stood below looking up at his dear Abba, who in that brief moment seemed like a complete stranger to him. Jezreels' gray hair flowed neatly, and his beard was soft and white like the snow on Mount Herman. That was Mishis' Abba, but here in this place it was as though he belonged to everyone else.

As Jezreel spoke his eyes searched the crowd for any responsive soul eager to make amends for wrongs they had committed. Then without warning his eyes caught sight of Mishi standing among the throngs. It was as though the sun suddenly stood in its place and time stopped. His mouth gaping, Jezreel paused in mid sentence. He gazed down at his son as if awaking from a dream, for the words of the prophet had now taken their flight.

In one swift motion he came down to Mishi and once again belonged only to him. Jezreel's large rough hands cupped his sons face as he knelt in from of him. "Mishi, what are you doing here, where is your momma, has harm befallen her?" he asked. Mishi could feel a huge lump forming in his throat as emotions flooded his soul, "she is safe Abba," he said, "but she has sent me to bring you home, for priests from the Temple are there, and they are inquiring about you."

Mishi watched as the blood raced away from his Abba's face making him white and pale. Then quickly standing upright and laying his giant hand in Mishi's, Jezreel turned and began leading him through the crowds. Few words were exchanged between them as they picked their way through the busy streets. The same thoroughfare that brought fear to Mishi as he traveled alone now looked less frightening with his Abba at his side. As he journeyed he felt a sense of pride, for he had served his mission and completed it. In his mind it wasn't man and boy passing through the busy streets, it was man and man.

When they arrived home Anna had already instructed the servant to wash the priests' feet and she had also served them tea and sweet cakes. They were sitting in the courtyard and when she saw Jezreel and Mishi arrive she exchanged a worried glance with her husband, and then quickly made the introduction.

"This is the master of our household," she said, extending her hand out toward Jezreel. At this the three priests arose and stood with little show of warmth or greeting. Anna continued with the introduction; "This is Hachmoni, Ebed-Melech, and Zadok, priesthood from the Temple. They desire to speak with you Jezreel." As she spoke these words Anna moved gracefully toward Mishi, retrieved his hand from his Abba, and led him aside. Mishi, who just moments before had felt so proud and fulfilled in his dutiful accomplishment now felt as though he was being transformed back into a child again.

It was Zadok the priest who was flanked by the two others which spoke first, "Are you Jezreel, son of Hosea the Prophet and Gomer his wife?" The question could not have been asked with any more formal tones or superior attitude. Jezreel immediately became defensive in his spirit, crossed his arms, and responded with the same arrogance; "I am!"

Zadok looked straight into Jezreel's eyes, unmoved by the challenge to his priestly authority. "Then you must come to the Temple with us at once, for a scroll has been found and the High Priest hereby summons you to appear before him." Jezreel could not believe his ears, "a scroll?" he asked, "but what does that have to do with me?"

At that moment all three of the priest turned and began to walk toward the gate in unison. "The High Priest will tell you everything," Ebed-Melech said, "now come, for we must be going." Then the priests stopped and waited for Jezreel to join them as though he had no other choice.

Mishi stood there holding his mother's hand, watching as his Abba joined the men and left with them. Jezreel did not speak goodbye, he simply left! Mishi's heart was pounding inside his chest, he could not understand how men from the priesthood who proclaimed goodness and righteous standards, could hold such power and control over them. "What power could cause his dear Abba to leave without as much as a goodbye to his own family?" he wondered.

Enraged, Mishi hurriedly broke away from his momma's hand and went scurrying up the steps attached to the side of their house. These steps led to the roof, where many family activities took place. From this lofty position the Temple was in distant view. The smoke from the daily sacrifice was always visible, ascending up to God. Many days he had stood here in awe and reverence at the scene. Today however, all he could feel was anger and confusion. He knew it wasn't right to allow such anger to rise within him, but for now he allowed it to wage a battle inside. It was fear for his father, fear of the unknown that lurked in the back of his mind. But it was the rage against the power wielded by these priests that flooded his heart.

He walked over and picked up a loose pebble that had fallen free from the protective wall surrounding him. He stood there rolling the smooth round weapon in his hand. Finally his anger overtook him and he threw the stone in the direction of the Temple. He did not know if the outcome from all of this would be good or bad; now it didn't matter! If the cold sovereignty of the priest portrayed how "holy" men behaved, then maybe, just maybe he would never have anything to do with them again. *"Had they thanked his momma for the cakes or for the servant washing their feet? Had they thanked him for fetching his Abba? No! They had just come and took his Abba away!"* Mishi turned in frustration and sat down with his arms resting on his knees and his back to the cool stones. "I know I should not act like this," he spoke out loud, taking a long resolute breath. He sat there for a long while overcome with emotion, searching inwardly for the godly man he longed to be, just like his Abba.

****

When Jezreel and the priests arrived at the Temple many people had gathered in the massive complex for afternoon prayers. By now the sun had warmed the normally cool flooring stones of the outer Gentile court. Upon entering the Temple precinct Hachmoni had stopped him, requiring him to remove his sandals before proceeding any deeper into the *Bet Hamakodesh.* This place, Hachmoni had told Jezreel, was; *"a House of Holiness."*

As the worshippers saw the four men approach they immediately opened a path for them. The priests flanked Jezreel as they moved across the platform, but Zadok walked ahead leading the procession. The Holy Temple loomed gloriously in front of them with its massive white stones glistening in the late afternoon sun. The smell of flesh burning on the altar filled the air around them. The priests led Jezreel through a gate on the south side of the Temple court and quickly through the hushed halls to a chamber deep within the maze of corridors. Inside, the stone flooring went cold against Jezreel's bare feet. He stood gazing around the room surrounding him; its circumference could have been no more than fifteen square feet. The oil lamps in wall niches cast suspicious tones to the atmosphere. The walls were smooth, almost like glass, as though they had been polished a thousand times. There was nothing else in the whole room but a single table set in the center, and on that table a small chest made of olive wood.

Zadok's voice echoed off the walls, startling Jezreel, "you may wait in here, the High Priest should not be long in coming," he said. Then all the priests left him with no further explanation. For a moment Jezreel was left alone, but not for long, for in just another moment Ebed-Melech re-appeared with a seat in hand. "I thought you might wish to sit down while you wait," he said; "I'll be right outside the door should you need anything." And with that Jezreel was finally and completely left alone.

He carefully positioned the seat in front of the table and sat down taking a long cleansing breath. His eyes were drawn immediately upon the small chest before him. He ran his finger gently across its lid, wondering if its contents could explain the reason for his being there. His mind whispered, *"open it,"* but his heart of goodness prevailed as he leaned back, slowly trying to relax and wait upon the High Priest.

Time passed so slowly that he could not tell just how long he sat there. The thoughts of what the chest could contain continued to race through his mind like wildfire. Suddenly he jumped and was startled back to reality by the entrance of the priests as they escorted a man in glorious attire into the room.

Zadok made the introduction, "Jezreel, this is Malchiah, High Priest over all the House of Israel." Although it was evident that Malchiah was a man of many years, somehow Jezreel also sensed the High Priest's countenance had been somewhat preserved as youthful. *"Maybe it is God's presence which has brought continual healing to him,"* he thought. Yet it was the aroma of incense which stood out in Jezreel's mind the most. The pleasant scent of cinnamon had filled the room the moment the High Priest had entered. Jezreel could imagine the High Priest being anointed with the holy oil, which was laced with cinnamon and other spices administered by the Apothecary. Malchiah wore a long robe ephod, wholly of woven work. The color was dark blue and it descended to his knees.

Jezreel quickly knelt and bowed in reverence, kissing the High Priest's feet. After a moment the High Priest reached down and touched Jezreel's shoulder, "rise up brother of the House of Israel," he said, with a voice that sounded like thunder. Jezreel arose, trembling as his eyes met once again with Malchiah's. He noticed that the other priests were moving, each finding a place against a particular wall. Malchiah sat in the chair, pulling it close to the table while motioning for Jezreel to walk around to the other side for their conversation. Jezreel now stood with the table between them as he faced the High Priest. Malchiah looked up at him and asked, "Jezreel, these priests have told me your father was Hosea the Prophet and your mother was Gomer his wife, is this correct?" "What the High Priest hath spoken is true," Jezreel said in carefully measured tones.

Zadok leaned over and handed Malchiah a key with which he unlocked the chest on the table. From the chest he retrieved a scroll and carefully unrolled it laying it out on the table. The smell of old leather drifted up, filling the room. Jezreel's eyes fashioned on the parchment which lay before him, and he knew this was the very object which surely must have caused all the disquiet of the day.

The scroll reeked of being ancient and musty. Its brown layers had been carefully rolled together and tied with a linen strip. The writing on the parchment was in the perfect scribe transcript, though worn from time.

As Malchiah's fingers carefully unrolled the scroll he began to speak; "a few days ago this scroll was found near the Gihon Spring. As workmen were cutting the rock for a water passageway, one of them discovered this scroll within a clay jar. Evidently it had been placed there for safe keeping by its scribe. The scroll bears the name of your father and mother. The priesthood has examined the scroll and felt it bears witness to The Word of The LORD."

Jezreel's heart leaped within him at the mere thought of having a scroll written by his father. He wondered what it could contain, especially since Malchiah had said the scroll also mentioned his mother.

Malchiah then continued, "There are some things, however, that are very troubling to us concerning the scroll. In his writings your father claims that The Word of The LORD came to him and instructed him to take a wife of whoredom, Gomer by name, your own mother." Malchiah stood and walked around to Jezreel as though attempting to convince him of the inexorability of the High Priest's words.

"Jezreel, you know this cannot be," the High Priest continued, "for it is against the commandments of God. We all know your father as a prophet, but to acknowledge that God prompted him to marry a wife of whoredom would surely confuse the people. And if we gave any acknowledgement from the priesthood that your father's writings were a holy script we are sure this would justify the nation's own adulterous and sinful ways."

Jezreel shook his head in disbelief. "I do not know all this scroll contains, but I know the heart of my father. His was not a life of justifying sin, but rather one of showing forth God's divine love, even to the outcast." Like the days when his father and mother had been alive and walked among the scorn of the people, Jezreel could feel the fires of resentment burn within him. He now sensed the glaring eyes of the priests in the room. He could suddenly hear the voices from long ago whispering disapproval and hatred as his family had walked the streets of Jerusalem. He felt again the sting of judgment and sensed the eyes of all Israel would be upon him.

Malchiah interrupted his tormented thoughts, "Jezreel, while this scroll contains many things challenging to our spirits, it is our purest desire to know God's perfect mind and will! May I ask you to come back tomorrow and rehearse for us the account of your father and mother? Tell us of this divine love you spoke about which your father showed to her. Perhaps your sharing their story will help us judge whether The LORD truly did speak to your father."

Jezreel could not speak; it was as though his tongue was swollen against the top of his mouth. All he could say was; "I shall see, after prayer, I shall see." He bowed again to the High Priest, sensing the conversation was over.

With that he turned toward the door, awaiting permission to leave. Zadok walked over and opened the door for him and led him back out into the courtyard. No words passed between them, Jezreel was lost in thought and oblivious to anything or anyone around him. He did not even look back at the glorious Temple, now illuminated by many lanterns which cast a golden tint to its stones.

Night had completely fallen as Jezreel made his way back up the hillside to his home. He could hear voices faint and soft from the houses as he passed. As he walked the narrow streets, a few times a friend or neighbor would call out to him from their roof, "Shalom Jezreel," but he never looked up, never returned the greeting. The stars and moon illuminated his path as he walked quickly with resolved steps, *"home, I just want to get home,"* he thought!

The house was silent when he arrived. Anna was mending one of Mishi's garments by lamplight in an attempt to ease her worried mind. When Jezreel entered the door Anna quickly jumped up and embraced him.

Her fingers traced the outline of his face while kissing his cheeks, and she noticed his eyes were moist with tears. Jezreel looked as though the weight of a thousand millstones had been placed upon his shoulders. Although Anna wanted desperately to inquire about Jezreel's visit from the priests, she asked him little, because the ears of a child were near.

Soon they were lying on their bed mats, and thinking Mishi was fast asleep, Jezreel begin to tell Anna all that had transpired. But sleep would not come too little Mishi. Even with his stomach filled with bread, figs, and honey, brought by Shekina, his mind still could not rest. He lay there listening to his Abba share the amazing yet sorrowful details of the priests' visit, and what happens in Israel when an ancient scroll is found. Yet after many restless hours and listening to Jezreel share all the day's happenings, Mishi finally drifted from the land of the living into a dream world, where boys become men.

Men like his dear Abba.

Chapter 2

Listen With Your Heart and Not Your Ears, Lest God Pass You By

The LORD instructed Hosea and said to him, "Go, and marry a promiscuous woman, have children by her, for like the adulterous wife you are to marry, this land is also guilty of unfaithfulness unto me."

Hosea 1:2

Standing outside the gate where just the evening before Zadok had led him through, Jezreel paced nervously. He ran his fingers through his thick gray hair as he waited to be ushered into the priestly chambers. His body ached from a long and restless night with little sleep. Anxious thoughts had invaded his mind as he prayerfully considered the great impact the scroll could have on his family and all of Israel. His anxieties did not lessen with the rising of the sun! Instead, those anxieties drove him from his bed mat and out into the courtyard of his home for early morning prayers. He knew what he must do, there was no other choice! He must return and defend his father and mother's names.

****

"I am sorry you had to wait," Hachmoni said as he unlocked the doorway. "Tomorrow we will provide you with a piece of fabric dyed purple. This will let the gate keeper know you have our permission to enter. Give it to him and he will bring you to us swiftly."

"*Tomorrow*" Jezreel thought, "I will not be here a day passed this one. I will plead my parents cause, ask for the scroll and return to my family."

Hachmoni did not lead Jezreel into the same chamber as the day before. Instead he was led into a much larger room, on the western side of the complex. The chamber rested just behind the actual Temple itself. Jezreel felt a sense of awe and holy reverence knowing he was only a stone's throw away from the Holy of Holies. That was the place designed specifically to house the *Aaron Kodesh*, Israel's Ark of the Covenant.

Upon entering the room many things were noticeably different. There were pillows to sit on, placed in an orderly fashion around the room. A table filled high with bread, fruits, and wine sat neatly tucked to one side. Jezreel's eyes searched the room for the chest that held the scroll, but it was not to be seen. Four menorahs, one in each corner illuminated the room with their brilliant light. Another door opened from inside the room, which Jezreel summarized, must surely lead to more interior chambers.

Hachmoni motioned for him to take his place on one of two pillows in the center of the room. "Did your soul find rest last evening?" Hachmoni asked, breaking the silence. Jezreel arranged himself on one of the pillows and answered him; "As well as one could expect, when his very world has been placed in sudden upheaval I suppose." Hachmoni gave a short sigh, folded his hands in front of him, and for the first time offered a faint smile of compassion for Jezreel. Hachmoni stood looking at him as though his eyes could read the very depths of Jezreels' soul.

In an effort to take the attention off himself Jezreel decided he would return the question, so he asked; "And you, my lord, did you find rest, and did your soul regain strength last night?" Hachmoni's smile widened, "ah yes, my soul found sweet peace and rest, but not until I had prayed a long time for you."

Jezreel studied him deeper now. Had this priest actually shown compassion and concern for him? For reasons not yet understood Jezreel sensed the distrust he had held within his heart for Hachmoni was slowly being washed away. Jezreel observed as Hachmoni walked over to the table laden with food and prepared a plate for him. Then Hachmoni gently placed the gracious gift in front of Jezreel, "Eat, my brother, you will need to be strong for the task ahead," he encouraged.

As the aroma of fresh baked bread, fruits, and wine awakened Jezreels' senses, he also felt a strange awareness of a distant, yet new acquaintance, a familiarity about Hachmoni which brought immediate comfort. Jezreel looked up at Hachmoni, "thank you my lord", he said, offering a smile which both men felt united them in a mutual knowledge of acceptance.

Soon the interior door opened and six men entered the room including, Ebed-Melch and Zadok. Each priest took their place without any instructions, as though they had done this many times before. Three of them sat on pillows with their backs to the wall on the right side of the room, and the other three likewise on the opposite side. Each one wore a long white robe with a wide blue belt. Their hair from under the white cap covering appeared neatly groomed, while each mans beard flowed long yet graceful. Once again the aroma of holy incense filled the room, having become deeply woven into the fabric of the priestly garments.

Malchiah soon appeared through the same interior doorway and with one voice all the priest proclaimed; "Blessed is the High Priest of Israel, Blessed art Thou oh LORD our God which made him holy, to perform atonement for sin!"

Malchiah walked over unmoved by the priest's proclamation and sat down beside Jezreel. Once he was comfortably arranged on the pillow, he spoke to the priests gathered in the room.

"Brethren, God has this day laid upon you the sovereign calling to hear and decide if the voice of The LORD hath spoken through the scribed words of the man called Hosea. Jezreel his son will rehearse his father's story before us! I bid you, listen with your heart and not your ears, lest God pass you by. Beware, for there are many things about the scroll in question that will challenge your soul, your mind, and especially your spirit!" Malchiah then extended his right hand to Jezreel, bidding him liberty to speak.

Jezreel felt the weight of truth heavy upon his shoulders as he began;

"I am glad that I shall speak for myself in this matter, but not for myself only, but for my beloved father Hosea, and my mother Gomer. For through them God hath shown His ever loving kindness to all the House of Israel, even to all of us sitting in this room. The power of that love was shown by the witness of my father's grace extended to a wayward wife."

Jezreel reached over and took a sip of the wine to wet his already dry parched lips as he continued.

****

"One day my father was by the Yarmulke River where crowds of people had gathered to hear the Word of The LORD. While he was prophesying of God's impending judgment some of the people asked; "what will God do with us, oh prophet of the LORD, if we do not turn from our sins, and in our hearts return to righteousness?"

Hosea spoke to them saying; "God who is longsuffering with you also requires that you turn from your wickedness and whoredoms. But God's mercy flows long and deep even to the outcast, like this river the Yarmulke."

He never could have foreseen how soon he would be faced with his own words, and challenged to obey God's voice. He was to be chosen by God to take upon himself the stain of sinfulness and to be identified with sinners. He never gave approval of riotous living, but rather showed God's tender mercy through his own obedience.

It was late the same evening as Hosea entered the city of Jerusalem, night had fallen and the streets were almost vacant. As is well known, few venture out after sunset for there is always much to fear in the darkened streets. His vigilant steps led him past many homes, where he could hear the low voices of families together, some peacefully singing an ancient psalm or hymn of Moses. The aroma of a late night meal being taken on the rooftop of a house he walked past awakened his own hunger. The delicious smell caused his mind to drift from its watchful state.

No sooner had these thoughts of hunger dulled his alertness than off in the distance he could hear the sound of weeping. The loud and mournful sobbing was like that of a grieving woman whose very heart had been ripped away from her. Hosea stopped, attempting to determine where this lamentation was coming from. He slowly turned to his right and walked carefully into a narrow alley following the wailing that penetrated out into the darkness.

As he drew closer his eyes caught sight of the shadowy image of a woman sitting in the corner of two crumbling walls. She sat bent over, her knees drawn tight against her chest. Her hands were cupped in front of her face to catch the flood of tears falling from her eyes. Her hair looked dirty and was stuck to her face as if serving as a veil from the world around her. Hosea stood there for a long time not exactly sure what to do. The lantern that hung from a rope in his hand cast shadows all around her.

Finally he spoke very tenderly; "why are you weeping, has someone hurt you, I am Hosea the Prophet, is there some way I can help you?" His voice had frightened her! She jerked back from him immediately, attempting it seemed to hide herself in the stone wall behind her. "Get away from me, what do you want from me?" She said, peering at him with eyes wild, and swollen with tears.

"If possible, I only wish to ease your pain," Hosea responded, almost apologetically from interrupting her right to sorrow. His words seemed to bring some curiosity to her spirit. Yet he sensed a recklessness about her that he was sure had never been tamed.

"You wish to ease my pain?" She asked, now half filled with pretentious laughter, and half with indignation. "Oh I am sure you do, just like every other man in the whole of Judea desires to ease my pain, with promises never fulfilled!"

Hosea stood there, not sure how to respond! He was a prophet and prophets it seems always have plenty to say. He twisted the rope holding the lantern out of nervousness, and his mouth was as dry as cotton. His mind was struggling how to respond.

Then he watched as her shadowy imagine began to move more into the light cast around them. She slowly extended her hand toward him as though she was expecting him to fill it with diamonds from Solomon's mines. "Well, what shall you promise me, my grand deliverer?" She asked, laced with sarcasm.

Hosea's mind raced for words! "Ah, I am but a prophet of the Lord, sent to speak love to the broken hearted, and hope to the castaway," he said, looking down with embarrassment at her forwardness.

With this she quickly bowed herself in front of him, "oh forgive me, great prophet of the Lord," she said mockingly, then, she spit upon his feet! Hosea watched as she arose and stood there glaring at him with renewed spite. "A prophet who speaks about love? Well I am sick of love," she said. "If God really cared about the outcast as you say, well, then why would he not heal the weariness deep within my heart? Why does he leave me to walk in my shame? Do you not understand what I am? I am a woman of the streets. I sell my body just to put food in my stomach! And you, with your righteous prophetic sermons dare tell me about Gods love and hope? I did not ask for this miserable life, and yet I am a prisoner of despair, enslaved to dreams that never really come true. Oh, but I have prayed, I have prayed more prayers than all the lips of the righteous, only to have them go unanswered!"

When she had finished speaking, both of them stood for a moment frozen with emotion. Hosea did not speak, he gave no rebuttal! Instead, he slowly removed two coins from the pouch around his waist and gently laid them on the ground in front of her.

"Tonight," he said, "you will need no slavery to another to fill your belly with bread." And with that he

turned and started to leave. Then a thought occurred to
him, so, he turned to her and asked; "may I know your
name, that I may pray for these dreams you have, that God
would answer them, and bring you love, real love?"

She knelt to retrieve the coins Hosea had placed at
her feet, but she never took her eyes off him. "My name is
Gomer," she said, through parched and broken lips. "And
my name means complete! But look upon me, for I am
anything but complete. Not only do all the eyes of Israel
scorn me, but my own name mocks me every time it is
spoken!"

Gomer walked past him, never thanking him for
the coins, his prayers, or concern. She just faded into the
night shadows.

Hosea stood there watching her until she was out
of sight. He attempted to bring himself to full
consciousness. "What have I done?" he asked himself.
"Have I sinned, by allowing myself to be enticed by the
beauty and emotions of this sinful woman? I am a man
given to holiness and purity! Perhaps someone may have
seen me with her and my righteousness evil spoken of."
He quietly and carefully made his way out of the dark
shadows and onto the roadway leading back to his home.

Trying as he might, he could not get her out of his
mind. Long into the night he lay restless, hearing her
words ring over in his ears.

"*I am sick of love,*" she had said. "*And you, with your
righteous prophetic sermons dare tell me about Gods love and hope?*"

His heart pounded deep inside. He had never felt
such compassion, such sympathy for anyone in all his life.

Where had it come from? He could not get the image of her tear stained faced out of his mind.

He tossed about on his bed mat, wondering if she had found a place of rest, or was she still shivering out in the coldness of the night air.

Finally, after many hours, he sat up, and in his heart, he could picture himself guiding her to his home and making a place for her by the fire. Perhaps he could at least take her some blankets to protect her against the cold.

Hosea shook his head. "You silly prophet," he said out loud, "what would people say if tomorrow they should pass by only to find a woman such as her kind in your home?" But all these thoughts did not quiet the restless worry in his mind. He could not, help her anymore this night! But his thoughts never left her, and sleep was long in coming.

The next morning he awoke with his mind filled with haze, his head aching with the sleeplessness of his restless night. He stood up, feeling the warmth of the morning sun on his face, rolled up his bed mat, and descended the stairs from his roof to collect wood for the morning fire.

The street outside his home was still peaceful as he walked quietly so as not to awaken anyone. The houses on his street were lined up so close to one another that one could travel the length of the road by stepping from rooftop to rooftop.

His neighbor saw him emerge and called down to him in a loud whisper from his roof where he was cooking the morning meal. "The Prophet was late in coming home last night wasn't he?" Hosea had attempted to forget his encounter, to dismiss the images of the tear-stained face from his mind for a while. But his neighbor's remarks brought the emotions and events of the night to him full force.

"Yes," he said, looking up with his eyes squinting into the morning sun. "The prophet was late in returning home, for you see God cannot always bring the sinner to himself in the light of day." But this was not enough to satisfy his friend, who often heckled Hosea good-naturedly.

"Ah yes he continued, but many a righteous man has been lost to temptation in the darkness of night."

"My friend," Hosea went on to explain. "The night holds no such dangers for me, for I am a prophet who keeps his eyes on the path ahead, even when that path is poorly lit," he said with a nervous laugh.

After the morning meal, Hosea made his daily journey to prayer. He had no particular place where he made petition unto the Lord. Some days he went to the Temple to join his fellow brethren, and others, such as this day, he simply followed wherever his heart might lead. This morning it led him on a distant path, across the Kidron Valley into an olive grove. It was a beautiful place. A place where one could empty his soul of all the burdens of the day.

The garden lay on the western slope of the Mount of Olives near its base. The smell of olive oil hung in the air as it was pressed from the fruit in the stone vats. The trees here were ancient, some perhaps a thousand years old. Their trunks twisted precariously, like the wrinkles of an old man's face. Oh the stories these trees could tell, of wars, and kings, and patriarchs whose feet had trodden under their branches.

Hosea knelt under some of the trees, allowing their limbs to serve as a canopy to cover his head from the quickly ascending sun. "Oh God of our fathers, God of Abraham, Isaac, and Jacob, hear this day the cry of thy servant Hosea. Forgive the sins of thy people Israel."

His soul was heavy as the wind rustled softly through the olive trees around him. Then without warning, the face of Gomer came again before his mind's eye. He began to weep uncontrollably for her. The Prophet pled her cause. "God I pray that she would come to know thy ever-loving kindness. Look upon her tears of sorrow and turn not thy face from her. Please redeem her unto yourself." His heart felt as though it would burst inside with compassion for her. After praying long, and his soul well spent, he rose saying, "thy will be done, in all things oh sovereign Lord, thy will be done."

For days thereafter, Hosea saw Gomer in every woman he met. As he walked through the market his eyes kept a constant vigil for her. Often, as he moved through the hoards of people around the city, he would hear a voice and his heart would race thinking that it was Gomer that spoke. Time after time though, he was disappointed.

As many days passed he slowly forgot about her. He thought of her less and less. Occasionally while drifting off to sleep, Gomer would enter his mind. "I wonder what ever happened to her, and if she found peace and love?" he would ponder.

Until one night as he lay upon his bed mat fast asleep, suddenly the Word of the LORD came to him in a vision, *"Hosea, go and take unto thee a wife of whoredoms and children of whoredoms; for the land hath committed a great sin, departing from the Lord."*

He awoke with a fright, considering for a brief moment that someone must surely be standing by his bed mat, and had spoken those words out loud and powerfully to him.

Hosea arose from his bed mat, with his mind and heart filled with great distress. He walked to the corner of his roof, peering out into the night, but there was no one there but him. "It must have been a vision, an angel, which has spoken unto me." He could hear his heart beating in his ears; his hands were sweaty, as tears began to stream down his face.

He tried to replay the angelic image in his mind as he stood there holding onto the railing surrounding his roof. But the image would not revisit his weary mind. It was the voice, and the words which so powerfully continued to reverberate over and over in his head.

Finally he looked up into the star lit heavens and prayed; "Lord, why do you bid me thus? Do you not understand that I will be made a laughing stock for thy name sake?" He stood there listening to the voices that fill the darkness, those which echo in complete silence, words only the wind speaks. He sat down and placed his feet upon the stone wall, realizing that sleep would not come for this night. He wrapped his cloak around himself for warmth, and let his mind drift. Gomer once again invaded his thoughts. Was it for this purpose that God had allowed their momentary encounter? Her face came before him, skin like ivory, hair black as the night surrounding him, and her eyes like the blue of the Mediterranean.

While sitting there that night a new kind of love entered his heart. One he had never known, or felt before. The last few weeks this love had enveloped him, called to him, and pursued him, like the wafting scent of some sweet smelling flower. He replayed her words in his mind, *"and what shall you promise me oh my grand deliverer?"*

Hosea spoke out loud to her, out into the echoes of night. "Maybe, just maybe I am your deliverer, and perhaps I shall teach you what love truly is." The tears that had dried in his beard drew his face tight, as a faint smile formed on his lips. Soon his eyes became heavy. He gave one last look toward the east and could see the faint glow of orange against the clouds hanging over Mount Olivet. "Yet but a little while and it will be daylight," he thought.

The sound of children's voices jolted him awake. Hosea sat upright, the sun had now risen, and in the street below children ran and played. He flung his cloak from around him, stood upright, and knew that his life from this morning forward would never be the same. "I will find her, my search shall begin today, and I will not stop until I fulfill God's command!" Quickly he descended the stairs with a whole new purpose to his life.

Chapter 3

A Friend within the Priesthood

"A man's wisdom gives him strength, and a man of knowledge seeks to grow stronger."

Proverbs 24:5

Jezreel's discourse had taken them late into the afternoon. Preparing to continue his story he looked around the room at his audience. He had become so engrossed in sharing the story of his parents, that Jezreel had not noticed how warm the room had gotten by the late afternoon sun. The priests had listened very closely to his discourse, but now seemed anxious and restless. Before Jezreel could begin the next chapter of his parent's narrative Malchiah's voice interrupted his thoughts. "My son let us all take bread, and wine and then you may return again on the morrow and share more of this interesting account with us," he said.

Soon a table laden with breads, fruits and meats was set before them. Jezreel looked at the feast, amazed at how quickly it had been provided. There were olives, cheeses, dates, figs, and of course bread. He summarized just from its appearance the meats consisted of both roasted lamb and beef. Jezreel realized he was actually partaking of priestly portions left over from the daily sacrifice. He was humbled to think the priests were allowing him to share with them as though he was one of their brother-hood. The food exchanged among them gave him strength, as his mind and spirit was weary from expounding such heavy words.

"I think your narrative will bring you back to us for many days," a voice spoke to Jezreel from over his shoulder. Hachmoni was standing behind him, with a cut cloth of purple color in his hand.

"Yes," Jezreel said, "I think you are right." Hachmoni gave him the purple cloth, saying, "don't forget my son, tomorrow when you arrive at the gate, give this to the keeper of the door and he shall bring you to us with swiftness." Jezreel took the cloth, carefully folding it, before stowing it safely in a fold of his tunic. "Thank you my lord, and may God shine upon you and bring you peace."

Hachmoni led him through the gate and into the Gentile Courtyard, whereupon he reached out his hand, extending it toward Jezreel. In it he held a sack, brown in color and with a small rope tied around the top. Jezreel accepted it from him with an inquisitive look, asking, "What is this, my lord?" Hachmoni's face showed once again the disarming smile that Jezreel had seen early that morning when the two of them had exchanged greetings. "Jezreel, I have prepared a small gift for you! Now go, for you must find rest. May the Lord bring you safely to us again in the morning!"

Jezreel watched as Hachmoni disappeared beyond the Temple gates. Then tucking the sack into his belt, he turned his steps toward the city, and to his beloved home.

When Mishi saw him coming up the pathway leading to their home, he quickly jumped up from his chore of trimming the flax wick for the lamps, and ran to meet him, his bare feet kicking up dust from the path. Jezreel's face showed a more pleasant countenance than it had the day before. Mishi took him by the hand and they walked together the last remaining steps. "Momma," he said when they reached the gateway of the courtyard, "Abba has returned to us."

"Yes my son I see this, how are you Jezreel my dear husband?" Anna moved beside him and softly kissed his cheek. Although she had asked nothing of her husband, Jezreel could see the questions burning in her eyes. "All is well," he told her softly. "My message was well received." Jezreel's voice always had a certain authority with it, but now Anna noticed it was rasp, as though he had talked long, and it had taken its toll upon him.

He was thankful to be in the safety and comfort of their home. While standing there his mind raced back for a brief moment to the splendor of the Temple he had beheld. He knew that few people had visited so deeply inside the inner chambers where he had been. Few had partaken of a priestly meal such as he had been invited to share. Still he summarized; "*The Temple in all its glory could bring him no more comfort than being in the sanctuary of his own home on this evening.*"

It was a meager dwelling, typical of most others within the city of Jerusalem. It had a small courtyard entrance which lay behind a stone wall. Immediately to the right was an animal pen for the livestock to be kept at night. Across from it in the courtyard was a covered sitting area with a table where meals could be taken. The actual house was little more than seven cubits by seven cubits. Inside it was dark and hot on most days; so many activities took place on the roof which consisted of rolled clay carefully packed over wooden beams.

Jezreel turned to sit down and suddenly remembered the small sack Hachmoni had given him. Retrieving it from his belt he gently placed it down on the ground. Then, positioning himself on a seat began to undo the cord tied around the top. Mishi scurried over and knelt on the ground in front of him. He sat looking up into his father's eyes, squirming with excitement as though a mighty treasure were about to be unfolded. "What's in the sack," he asked, watching Jezreel's hands excitedly. Jezreel reached over and patted the top of his head, "be patient my little son and we shall see." Reaching inside, Jezreel removed other smaller bags, all tied in the same fashion. One by one he began to open their contents. The first held spices from the temple, such that Jezreel knew was of precious worth. Next they discovered some coins, enough to provide bread for his journeys to and from the temple each day. Finally the last treasure was slowly revealed.

Jezreel's posture straightened.

He sat looking down into his hand, and his face showed great confusion. In his hand he held a *signet seal*, a device used to stamp one's name into clay.

He sat there running his fingers over the letters, as his eyes filled with tears. Mishi could not keep silent one moment longer, "what does it say Abba, what does it say?"

"It is the name of my father Hosea," he said, still deep in thought.

"Where could Hachmoni have gotten this from?" he wondered aloud. *"Could it have been found with the scroll?"*

Even if it had been found with his father's writings, why would Hachmoni entrust it to Jezreel now? But the seal held no answers to the questions that burned in his head, only the name Hosea, could be read in the etching! Mishi watched as Jezreel carefully tucked the seal back into the bag for safe keeping. He arose and went inside the house, with Mishi following his every step.

"What does the seal mean Abba?" he asked.

Jezreel gently picked up his little son and held him in his arms, "It means that God is watching over us, my son. He has provided within the priesthood someone we can trust. For some reason Hachmoni has shown us favor. At this time, that is all I know, but it is enough."

Jezreel gave his son a wink, and sat him down on the floor. Mishi smiled, "I think I like Hachmoni," he said. Jezreel carefully placed the bag high up on a shelf just out of reach of Mishi's hands. "I think I like him too," Jezreel said, "now come it is time for bed."

When they awoke the next morning, some of the men from the community had gathered, demanding that Jezreel tell them why the priests had come asking for him. Anna had told him there had been many in the community asking questions in his absence. "Many are beginning to talk," she said. "They are fearful that your sermons at the gates of our city have inflamed anger from the priesthood."

At Anna's bidding, to keep peace within the community, Jezreel went out to meet with the men now gathered at his doorstep.

When he stepped outside into the morning sunlight, the small crowd of men fell silent. As he approached them, Ira, who seemed to be the leader of the group, spoke out; "Shalom Jezreel," he said with a false cheerfulness. "We have come to inquire about your dealings with the priesthood. You see, we don't want our peaceful community to be set in upheaval. But it seems you are creating trouble for us in the Temple!"

Jezreel threw his arms into the air with disappointment that these men, these brothers of their community, could so quickly allow distrust against him and his family to enter their hearts.

"Brethren, you know that for many years my heart has been to serve you and to show goodness and favor to all of you. I ask you now to trust, only trust. These priests mean you no harm; they have simply come inquiring about the writings of my father, Hosea. Neither I nor anyone among us know what God shall bring forth in this matter."

But the people would not be quieted. Ira, looking to his backers for support responded, "You ask for trust, yet you give no evidence of your good intentions. In this matter, we do not trust you, nor will we allow you to bring trouble upon our families!"

Jezreel had listened long enough, his anger began to boil. "I demand you leave us be at once, we have done nothing against any of you. I must be going now, peace be unto you my brethren." He drove a path between them, leaving them to shout their indignation at his back as he walk down the roadway leading away from his home.

It wasn't long after he had departed that Shekina arrived. With a voice that could move mountains she dispersed the crowd immediately! After all the people had gone, she went into the house, finding Anna and Mishi on the roof. "Never mind those meddling fools," she said. "Anna, God has his hand upon you, and he will bring honor to your household."

Jezreel walked as quickly as his feet could carry him. The encounter with the men had delayed him on his way to the Temple. He was fearful the priest would think he was not returning. He had hoped to arrive early today, not late. He wanted to inquire of Hachmoni about the signet seal, and to thank him for his gifts. He was soon walking up the long stairway leading from the lower city up to the giant platform where the Temple sat. There were few people walking about though the courtyard. His mind quickly summarized that, with the eve of Passover coming on the morrow, many would wait until then to come for worship.

As he approached the gate entrance, he saw the keeper awaiting his arrival. "Shalom," Jezreel said, as he lifted his outer cloak, looking for the purple cloth. The keeper greeted him with a familiarity, "Yes, my son

Shalom unto you! The priests were becoming anxious about your arrival." Jezreel looked up at him, "I was delayed in coming, but I am prepared now to meet them whole heartily."

Jezreel presented the purple cloth, and was taken inside.

The priests were already sitting in the chamber as he was ushered in. All stood and greeted him. Their warm welcome comforted his already troubled spirit. But he knew that these men who might show kindness because the law required it, could also in the same breath, pierce your very soul with judgment and harshness.

Before Jezreel could find Hachmoni among the men gathered, hoping to inquire of the signet seal and thank him for his gifts, Malchiah appeared. Each man took the same position as the day before, upon the pillows provided.

"We are thankful that God has brought you back to us again today, and we are prepared to hear more of the account of Hosea your father," Malchiah said.

With boldness and a determined spirit Jezreel cast his eyes around the room and spoke saying, "I am compelled by the Lord to share more with you concerning God's call to my father. This is the only reason I am here, because I am moved by His Spirit to proclaim the truth."

The High Priest said nothing, but gave consent by a simple bow of the head. Jezreel breathed a deep sigh, and once again proceeded with the defense of his beloved father Hosea.

Chapter 4

Oneness with Humanity

"God caused Him who had no sin to become sin for our sakes, so that, through Him we could be transformed into the righteousness of God."

2 Corinthians 5:21

Hosea wandered through the busy market place aimlessly picking up a piece of fruit holding it in his hand, and then laying it down again. Normally he would have been at his regular place, by the river Yarmulke and preaching on this day. But somehow his heart was just too heavy to preach! He felt disoriented and confused with all the new emotions that ran wild in his spirit. He had always felt such passion about the Word of God, and sharing what he believed the Spirit was impressing upon his heart. Now, it was as though all the fires that had burned within him for the Word of the Lord, had been harnessed in a mighty yoke, and was pulling him toward Gomer.

As he wandered through the market deep in thought, a hand came down upon his shoulder stopping him in his tracks. "The crop is good, good enough for even a prophet such as you," a friendly and familiar voice said. Hosea lifted his head to see the bright smiling face of Ishtob the market keeper. "You always know how to bring my heart joy," Hosea said. "You are a good merchant, perhaps I shall buy all the produce you have here!" Both men broke into laughter.

Ishtob was the kind of man that everyone loved. He had owned that market as long as Hosea could remember. *"Even his eyes smile,"* Hosea thought; glad to see his old friend. "You are a good man," Hosea said, "Not a greater man have I ever met than you."

Ishtob, was embarrassed by Hosea's flattery and inquired of him. "And just what have I done to receive such a high commendation from the prophet of the Lord? I rarely go to the house of the Lord. Nor have I been to hear the prophet speak these mighty tidings of repentance." But Hosea would not be discouraged from placing honor upon his beloved friend, so he continued his blessing. "But the merchant is filled with honesty, and uprightness. Many people have shared their troubles with you, and found guidance by your advice."

The market continued to fill with customers as the two men stood in conversation. It felt good to Hosea to relax for a little while and share laughter, and renew his friendship with Ishtob. They became so engrossed in conversation that neither of them realized how many people were mingling about in the little market. It seemed everyone in Jerusalem had arrived on the same day to buy from the good man Ishtob. As Hosea stood with his back to the throngs of customers, ready to share one more story with his friend, a voice from behind him caught his attention. It was a voice that seemed familiar, and one that he had played over and over in his mind.

He turned to see Gomer, there in the market, the very market he now stood. His heart began to race within him and it didn't take him long to forget the good man Ishtob and their conversation. In a captivated state of mind he began to walk toward Gomer.

She was examining some figs, unaware of Hosea's presence. Unabashed, he spoke as joy overcame him. "Gomer, is it really you? How wonderful it is to see you! I have been praying with great sincerity concerning your request of the Lord. I have asked Him to send you a man who will truly love you!"

By now the busy market had gone silent as everyone stopped and glared at them. Gomer cast her eyes upon Hosea, trying to remember who he was. After a moment or so it came to her; *"he was the prophet she had met only a few nights before."* Immediately, upon this revelation she became red faced, and embarrassed, that he would openly announce any previous discussion between them.

She quickly turned her back to him and started rummaging through the fruits and vegetables as she said quietly, yet sternly and under her breath; "as you have prayed for many wandering souls, I am sure." Then she moved to the other end of the stand trying to get as far from Hosea as possible and remove the focused attention from herself.

But Hosea followed her every step of the way. "In my heart, I have thought only of you every day, I have wished to know if you were safe." Hosea continued, "If I had but known where to find you deeper into the night of our first encounter, my compassion would have bid me, come to you and provide a place for you, one of shelter and warmth."

Gomer stood there gazing at him in complete disbelief of what her ears had just heard. "You are a crazy man and a crazier prophet. I need nothing from you, now let me be! I have more men in Israel that will give me shelter and warmth, than you have sermons in that mouth of yours."

But Hosea would not be deterred, "and just where had all these men gone, the night I found you cold and shivering and weeping in the loneliness of betrayal?"

With this, Gomer put her basket down and gave Hosea one swift push, sending him falling into the arrangement of produce. He now sat in the mist of overturned tables, of vegetables, and a harvest of ripened pomegranates all around him. Then, through his blinking eyes and to his complete surprise, he watched as she wheeled about and left him sitting in his awkwardness.

The next sound he heard was that of Ishtob, who was now laughing so hard that tears were streaming down his face. Walking over and leaning down to assist his fallen client he said, "that woman has the heart of a lioness, I doubt Samson himself could have tamed her."

"You know her?" Hosea asked, while brushing himself off and apologizing for all the disarray of merchandise. "Well of course I know her, haven't I been a merchant here for many years? She is Gomer, the daughter of Diblaim, a seller of figs. Many times I have purchased figs from her vineyard. Diblaim is a good woman, honest and filled with integrity. But Gomer is far removed from the ways of her mother."

Then he gave Hosea a curious look. "And just why may I ask would the good prophet Hosea be enquiring about a woman of her kind?" Embarrassed, yet deeply heavy with the calling in his heart Hosea could only answer, "because the Lord has put her deep within my heart Ishtob, that is the only way I know to answer you."

Ishtob continued to clean off the juice stains from Hosea's garments and began to speak as though he himself were the prophet and Hosea a retched sinner needing chastisement. "You best know that it is God that bids thee to enquire of her. She would think nothing of taking your life in the darkness of night while you sleep, with a dagger through your heart. This woman is the cause of many a man going astray from goodness and holiness. Trust me; her bed is the gate to hell!"

Hosea would not be moved from his quest by the words of his self-appointed adviser. He asked now with even more sincerity, "tell me Ishtob, where does she live, that I may find her? I am compelled to show her the ways of God, and what love from a heart of godliness can bring."

Ishtob, seeing he would not dispel the very intention of Hosea's spirit conceded the information he desired. "She has no continual dwelling, but can be found near the broad wall where many people go in and out of the city. For there she has many lovers, and enemies! Men who have stolen her very body and spirit from the family of godliness she once knew."

Ishtob placed both hands on Hosea's shoulders so he could look straight into his eyes as he continued to counsel him. "You will find her there among those men, but please Hosea, be careful, for she has cast the stone of hatred into many hearts. Her seeds of wickedness have ripped families apart, and caused much hostility for her. There are those who would take her very life away if they but knew God would forgive them."

Hosea was already moving toward the edge of the market as he spoke, "thank you Ishtob, I will be watchful because of your kind advice." Hosea promptly left with his purchase of fruit in hand. But he also carried with him the stain of his rendezvous with Gomer, which covered his garments.

He waited until the darkness of night to make his journey up to the area of the broad wall. It was a part of Jerusalem that sat North West of where Hosea lived, and was heavily populated. Hoards of people passed this way, and the wickedness to be found there had sent many a man to destruction. A mixture of both rich and poor occupied the cluster of homes attached to this walled extension of the upper city.

"And just how do you think you are going to find her?" Hosea said to himself as he walked through the maze of people. "Besides even if you do find her, you will probably end up dodging the swing of her hand, *you crazy prophet*," he said, mocking Gomer's words.

He was surprised to find the streets filled with people at this hour and especially after dark. He stopped and watched as a drunken man staggered past him, reminding him of Ishtob's warnings. Ahead of him he could see a festive celebration going on. There was singing, laughter, and plenty of dancing.

Hosea asked a passerby, "what is all the commotion?" "It's the last night of a wedding festival," the woman called back as she danced away. Hosea continued ahead, positioning himself upon the ledge of the broad wall, so he could watch the joyous occasion.

He seemed to enjoy the atmosphere, and thought this strange. He had always been one to steer away from such festive affairs. It was not that he didn't enjoy the fellowship of others; it was simply that years ago he had resolved himself to a life of celibacy, for the word of God's sake.

But tonight the air around him felt different and strangely enough, he felt comfortable here, among such a celebration. Now in fact he longed for it, and for the first time in his life he desired to know how it felt, to be married like everyone else. It was as though he had come down from the high and lofty position of prophet, to be one with the people. He had condescended, sharing both their joy, and sadness, but simply to be a part of them. Oh it wasn't that he desired to partake in any sinful acts, it all just seemed new to him, having lived for so many years isolated as a prophet and so devoted to holiness.

As he sat there, no one that danced around him even knew who he was. No one expected anything from him, no sermon, no words of guidance, or counsel. He knew he would preach again, and he knew he would once more feel the fire burn in his heart from the Word of God. But for tonight, he was just one with humanity.

After many hours the crowd grew weary from dance and song, and the streets started to clear. It was late and Hosea concluded that tonight he would not find Gomer. Preparing to dismount the ledge which had served as his window into this strange and new world, he peered down the street and could not believe his eyes.

Coming up the street was Gomer, attempting with all her might to lead a donkey, who was not very willing to cooperate. Hosea quickly hid behind part of the wall to observe this spectacle. He watched as she positioned herself facing the donkey and pulling it along. She was leaning back and tugging on the rope with all her might, cursing and swearing with every laboring step.

Gomer certainly could put forth more words in one breath than ten prophets all at the same time. Her back was to Hosea as she and her beast of burden drew near to his secret position. Hosea slipped back out onto the wall, with his legs dangling over the edge. He was smiling widely, as one awaiting a gift that was about to be presented to him on a silver platter.

When Gomer arrived in front of him, her eyes caught sight of her audience. She stopped in complete exhaustion and blurted out sarcastically; "oh, once again my grand deliverer!"

Hosea remained atop his seat of elation. "Where in the world did you get your new found friend?" He asked with a small chuckle. "Very funny," Gomer retorted. "The donkey is a gift from a man who had no money to pay for my love."

She once again attempted to get the donkey to follow her, but he wouldn't budge. He stood, firmly planted in his tracks.

Hosea could not help himself; he just had to stifle a laugh. He sat atop the ledge, his arms folded across his chest, and feeling like the prince of some grand kingdom which he had just inherited. "And shall thy grand deliverer assist this damsel in distress?" he asked.

At this, Hosea was sure he witnessed a faint smile on Gomer's face. It was a smile of surrender, of knowing that she was without choice. "And just how would you suggest that we persuade this rebellious animal?" Gomer asked. Hosea carefully slipped off his edifice of supremacy and walked over to them. He patted the donkey gently on the head. "We shall persuade him through leading not pulling."

He then retrieved fruit purchased earlier that day at the market. Hosea held it in front of the donkey's mouth and began slowly walking forward. The donkey immediately responded and followed Hosea's every step.

Gomer trailed in behind, not yet willing to consent defeat. Hosea looked back over his shoulder and asked; "So, exactly where were you going, and do you have a place to stay tonight?"

He heard Gomer speak from behind him with softness in her voice. "I wasn't really sure," she said. "My main concern was to get this dumb animal to a place of safe keeping until I can sell it. I could sleep on the ground if I had to, for out here you learn to survive." Her speech and the sound of her voice betrayed her. Hosea sensed that she was beginning to weaken her defenses!

"I know a place already prepared for you, a place that you can sleep and find warmth from the coldness of the night air." He spoke tenderly. Gomer laughed somewhat defiantly, "oh I am sure you do, you seem to think that you have just about everything I need. And where might I ask would this place of refuge be?"

Hosea stopped walking; he stood looking at her with eyes filled with compassion. Then in a gentle and inviting voice he said, "you can stay at my house, there you will be warm and protected from any evil that might lurk out here in the darkness. I will sleep elsewhere."

Hosea awaited her indignant response, but there was none. Gomer stood there frozen by generosity! She hardly knew what to say. Finally she broke the silence, "and what about this dumb animal where will he sleep?" Both of them let out a laugh. "Oh I am sure we will find a place for him. He is probably tuckered out after the way you were pulling and tugging on him." Gomer gave Hosea a playful slap of the hand as they turned their steps toward the home of the Grand Deliverer.

When they arrived at Hosea's house of refuge he put his finger to his lips and whispered softly, "shhhh, be very quiet we don't want to wake the neighbors." Gomer's eyes widened, "it's the dumb donkey you better be telling that to," she whispered back.

Hosea tied the beast of burden up outside in the courtyard and showed Gomer where she could find rest. He built a fire in the clay oven and placed a nice clean bed mat right in front of the warm glow. After straightening one last wrinkle in the mat, he proceeded to the doorway; "I will be right next door, if you should need anything."

Gomer waved him off with her hand, "stop making over me so, have you forgotten that I am the same woman who just this afternoon defended herself by shoving her assailant into a fruit stand?" "Ah yes, I do remember," Hosea whispered, pretending to flinch out of fear. "I don't think you will need worry about him attempting anything tonight." Hosea quietly slipped out the door, leaving her to find rest.

He walked the few steps to his friend's house. This was the same friend who enjoyed teasing and heckling him so much. He was the same friend who had questioned Hosea about being out late into the night, the night he had found Gomer, crying in the darkness. Hosea knew there would be many more questions to answer as he knocked on the door.

"Hosea, what are you doing out at this time of the night?" His friend asked. "I need to stay here with you until morning, my dear brother." Hosea said, now standing in the doorway pitiful like, as he awaited the barrage of questions.

He had never seen his friend at this time of the night and thought it funny how his hair was in complete disarray, and his eyes looked weak and bloodshot from having been awakened.

In a sleepy tone his friend asked; "but why, what prevents you from your own home of peace?" To quite him, Hosea reached up and placed his hand over the mouth of his friend. "Let's just say I found a stranger that needed refuge, and I permitted her to stay there."

He could see the eyes of his friend widen, as he carefully removed Hosea's hand, now allowing him to speak. "Her?" He asked with a faint smile on his face. "Did you say her?" he asked again.

"Yes her," Hosea whispered louder, "now can I please come inside, lest the chill of the night air, give all my secrets away?" The friend then moved to the side of the doorway and gestured with his hand, inviting Hosea in like a king entering his royal court. "Oh certainly you can stay, we couldn't have the secrets of the mighty prophet Hosea given away by the whispers of darkness, now could we?"

Chapter 5

You Cannot Kill the Glory of God

"And the glory (shekina) of the Lord will be revealed, and everyone will see it together; because the Lord has spoken it."

Isaiah 40:5

Jezreel's words were interrupted by the doorway of the inner chamber being opened. A priest entered the room that Jezreel had never seen before and moved quickly to the high priest. He did not give any apology for interrupting the dialogue. He leaned over, so as not to allow anyone else within the room to hear his words, as he whispered in Malchiahs ear.

All movement within the room stopped as everyone focused their attention on this unexpected visitor. They could tell immediately by Malchiah's expression as he listened intently, that this bidding, whatever it was, could be serious.

After what seemed an eternity, Malchiah stood and spoke; "Brethren we must conclude for the day is far spent." He then assisted Jezreel to his feet and asked to see him in private. Both men moved through the inner chamber doorway, into a hall that seemed to lead back under the Temple house itself.

When they were to themselves Malchiah stopped and turned toward him, his expression showed deep concern. "Jezreel, you must stay here tonight, for we have learned that certain men have purposed in their hearts to harm you," the High Priest said. Jezreel felt his body go weak with worry. "What men, and how did you learn this?" He asked.

Malchiah knew Jezreel deserved an answer even if he could not tell him everything. "There are certain men who have set themselves against the priesthood, and anyone whom they believe takes fellowship with us, immediately comes under the sights of their bow. These men know not why you are here, and to them it doesn't matter. They have already conceived imaginations in their hearts that you are conspiring with us. They do not need any other reason to despise you! Just knowing you are here is enough to cause their hatred to boil."

Jezreel's mind left the Temple and his own safety and went immediately to his family. "What about my son Mishi, and my wife Anna, do you know if they are safe?" Malchiah placed his hand on Jezreel's shoulder; "Temple advisers have already been sent to secure their safety. They shall be brought here to the Temple as soon as possible."

Jezreel turned away from the High Priest and walked a few steps attempting to gather his thoughts and his composure. He could feel tears welling up in his eyes. His heart was pounding in his chest! "Breathe, Jezreel, just breathe," he whispered to himself. He turned and faced Malchiah again. Walking over to him, he took the High Priest by the arm. "Please sir, I beg you, let no harm come to my beloved family, for, I shall not rest until I see their faces."

Malchiah did his best to comfort Jezreel but to little avail. The two men walked together deeper into the chambers of the massive Temple Precinct. If it could have been another time and under difference circumstances Jezreel would have been captivated by the beauty and architecture of this Holy Place. But for now all he could think about was his family's well-being.

When the advisers arrived at the home, and explained the impending danger, Anna and Mishi were instructed to gather as few belongings as would be needed for the journey. They promised to bring them to Jezreel swiftly, and with every protective measure necessary.

Anna asked if she might run to Shekina's to bid her farewell until they returned. But the men would not permit it. "We must move as quickly as possible," they said. When all was prepared and made ready, they began the journey.

They had only gotten to the edge of the courtyard when Anna suddenly stopped and ran back into the house. She returned carrying the brown sack that

Hachmoni had given Jezreel. "It could be that your father might have need of this," she said to Mishi, as they began their journey again.

Mishi was never so afraid, as that night. It seemed that the very trees and limbs reached out to take them captive as they walked. They wondered if they would ever see their home again. The last few days had torn their whole world apart and Mishi began to cry as the light from their home faded in the distance far behind them. Anna slipped her arm around his shoulders, to comfort him. "Mishi, we must be brave, God will somehow show his mighty power. He will protect us according to His perfect will," she said. Mishi looked up into his mother's loving face as he gave a soft smile. They were both glad to be going to where Jezreel was, even if it meant leaving their home. Mishi knew he would soon be able to feel his dear Abba's strong arms wrapped about him, and then all would be well.

As they approached the Temple complex the night torches gave a faint yellow glow on the pavement of the courtyard. The huge pillars inside the portico stood like soldiers, having been placed there to serve as their protectors. Perhaps it was the quietness surrounding the Holy Temple at this late hour of the night which brought a calmness that flowed over them both that neither could ever explain. It was as though one greater than all the mountains surrounding Jerusalem was now walking with them.

Arriving at a gate, they were forced to wait while one of the advisers conversed with the keeper of the door.

A breeze passed over Mishi and made him shiver in the night air as he also gave a tired and nervous yawn.

"You may enter," the keeper said as he led them inside. Mishi's eyes blinked attempting to focus in the dimness of light provided by the single lantern held by the overseer. They were quickly led to the chamber where Jezreel was waiting and when the door swung open Mishi ran to Jezreel and leaped into his arms. They all cried as Jezreel held on to them. "I am so glad you are here and safe with me now," he said.

Mishi sat there wrapped in his father's arms, feeling warm and comforted as Jezreel began to explain to them how his discourse was interrupted late into the afternoon by the priest who had entered. Anna asked him many questions as to what he knew regarding the potential dangers for their family. Jezreel was attempting to reassure her of God's divine sovereignty when a soft knock on the door broke their conversation.

Jezreel opened the door to find Zadok standing before him. "The brethren of the priesthood has sent you some food, and to offer you our prayers," he said as he looked past Jezreel seeing his family. Then he bowed his head in apology. "It was not meant to be this way, I am sorry that you have been caused grief by the thoughtless actions of a few insurgents," Zadok said. Jezreel carefully laid his hand on the priest shoulder. "Thank you Zadok, we are in God's hands, let Him do with us what he will."

Zadok assisted Jezreel in placing more furnishing in the small room that would serve as their home away from home. Wash basins made of bronze and as shiny as any Jezreel's family had ever seen were brought in. A small table and chairs were also supplied along with oil lamps and jars of olive oil. But it was three very thick and deliciously warm bed mats which caught tired little Mishi's attention the most.

As Zadok laid them out on the floor, Mishi, eager to try one, quickly ran over and laid down on it, giving out a sigh of pleasure. Zadok chuckled at the sight of him. "I am glad you like it son, I hope it will bring you good rest tonight."

Zadok bid them Shalom and turned to leave, and then in curious fashion he stopped at the door. "I think you should know; it was Hachmoni, which asked me to bring you the food and all these necessities. For some reason it seems his very heart is knit with you in deep and prayerful concern."

"Hachmoni has shown me grace and care from the time I first arrived here," Jezreel responded. "I will do my best to express my appreciation to him when given the opportunity."

"Good night, Shalom to all your family," Zadok said tenderly, as he turned once again to leave. Jezreel stood there in the doorway until Zadok was out of view; slowly he closed the door, and sat back down with his family. They were all hungry and set about examining the food which had been brought. As they ate the delicious warm meal they conversed about the events that had brought them there.

With their hunger now put to rest, it wasn't long until sleep began to creep into the room. Mishi's eyes became heavy and he slowly moved from the table and lay down on the warm bed mat. He watched the flickering light on the ceiling from the oil lamp as he listened to Anna and Jezreel talk softly. He could hear her tell Jezreel that she had brought the bag Hachmoni had given him. He heard Jezreel tell her he was glad she brought it. Finally the warmth of the covers against Mishi's skin prevailed as sleep took over his mind and body.

The early morning came with a loud rap on the door of the chamber. Mishi sat up on the mat and watched as his father stumbled to open the door. "Jezreel, may I enter your room?" the voice asked. Mishi recognized it to be the voice of Zadok. "Yes my lord you may enter," Jezreel bid.

When Zadok came into the room, he looked as though many years had passed, although it had only been a few hours since he had brought the food and other items. His hair was in disarray, and his eyes looked as though he had not slept at all. He immediately sought out a place to sit down. Anna wrapped a covering around herself and moved over to where Mishi had been laying and wrapped the covering around him also. Then the room went silent as they all waited for what Zadok had to share with them so early in the morning. He looked down at the floor so as not to catch eyes with any of them as he spoke in a broken voice. "There has been a terrible tragedy. Last evening after you were taken from your home, those with intention to harm you went to your house. But of course you were not there! However, a friend of yours, a woman of elder years had come to defend your cause. She encountered these men and attempted to send them away."

Zadok then stopped as though he wished not to continue. Anna gasp out loud in a concerned voice. "Oh Jezreel, it cannot be, these men have laid harm to Shekina!" Jezreel carefully went over and sat down with Anna comforting her. Zadok shook his head sorrowfully. It seemed to take all his strength to continue. "One of our advisers found her, thrust through with a sword; she had no life breath within her." Anna fell onto Jezreels shoulder, and wept great tears of sorrow at the thought of her dear friend's death.

It was late into the afternoon before Anna could hardly speak to them. Her sorrow was greater than any she had ever known. Jezreel stayed by her side attempting to comfort her, although her grief could not be healed. He gave no thought of continuing his discourse with the priest that day; instead, they permitted Jezreel and all his family to simply rest, and grieve the loss of their dear friend.

As the day wore on and the sun began its decent into the western sky, Jezreel began to feel the need of prayer and worship. It was also the beginning of the Sabbath, and "if they had ever needed worship and to be in God's presence it was now," he whispered to Anna.

Every hour or so one of the priests would gently knock on the door and ask if they needed anything. As evening approached, Jezreel inquired of them as to how they might observe the Sabbath meal. He was told that all would be arranged for them, they need not worry.

Evening began to fall and they were ushered into a dining room, and bid as guests to take the Sabbath meal with the men from the priesthood. Mishi's eyes lit up for he had never seen so much food in one place before. The mood, though somber, still had an awe of holy reverence and worship to it. The long table was surrounded by many priests all dressed in clean white robes. Jezreel and his family were placed on the right side and among the priests. Mishi watched carefully as the Sabbath lamps were lit and many prayers were offered. Anna tried to join the recitations but the words escaped her. All she could think about was Shekina and how she would miss her.

Malchiah, who sat at the end of the table, rose from his seat and delivered a discourse about the holiness of the day. And that on the morrow all people throughout the land of Israel and Judea would find renewal and faith, through the Sabbath provided by The Lord Our God. As he spoke Anna prayed silently that somehow God would renew her faith and bring the strength she so desperately needed.

As they walked back to their chambers, Mishi walked in between his parents holding both of their hands. "Abba, did you enjoy the meal tonight?" he asked. "Yes my son, it brought my soul faith and my body strength." Jezreel tenderly responded. Mishi looked up into his Abba's eyes as they continued to walk, "I don't feel angry at the priests anymore, how come?" he asked. Jezreel stopped walking and softly knelt in front of his little son. He placed his hand on Mishi's heart, "the reason you feel different is because you are carefully being transformed into a man, a man with a heart after the likeness of God."

Jezreel always kept before Mishi the fact that soon he would come to Bar Mitzvah; the time when a boy becomes a man. Mishi's face lit up with his Abba's approval, "I love you Abba, I love you Momma," he said as he wrapped his arms around Jezreel's neck.

When they arrived back in their chamber Anna began to question if Jezreel would continue with the priest after the events within their community, and the death of Shekina. "I must continue," he said with earnest, "if I don't then she will have died in vain. Her whole life and death has been to protect the truth and to preserve it. I am more persuaded now in my spirit than ever, that God has a purpose in all that is happening."

Jezreel walked to the door as though he was going to open it, but he just stood there lost in deep thought. "What does her name mean Abba?" Mishi asked. It was as though his words suddenly brought Jezreel back into the room from the place his mind had taken him. Though he did not answer Mishi, he stood with an expression on his face of great revelation. Like when one comes to understanding about a deep thought that has perplexed them for many days. Jezreel looked at Anna as if imparting the same revelation to her. After only a moment Anna's face lit up with a glow of joy as she spoke, "the visible glory of God, that's what Shekina means my son, the visible glory of God."

Jezreel came over and sat by him, laying his hand on Mishi's knee and spoke to him. "And we have beheld it; we have seen God's visible glory through Shekina's life and now her death. Her love for Him, and his holy word, was so great that it moved her with such passion for the truth that she gave her life for it." Jezreel paused as if allowing the next level of revelation to flood his soul, "but you cannot kill the glory of God! Shekina will live forever in the presence of her beloved God Almighty!"

Jezreel paced around the room as he continued to speak out into the air. "It is now but my reasonable service that I continue in proclaiming the truth concerning God's love through my father Hosea. I shall not waver until I have made all Israel to know of God's faithfulness, and of his loving covenant to all mankind!"

Chapter 6

Animosity Transformed Into Love

"My heart is sealed with deep love for you; I have written your name on my flesh; for love is powerful as death, its determination sure as the grave. Love burns in the heart like blazing fire, like a raging inferno."

Song of Solomon 8:6

When Hosea awoke the next morning, he quickly went about making the morning meal. His friend followed him around asking about this new house guest. As Hosea gathered wood for the fire he told his friend, "Her name is Gomer, and, I am fearful to tell you this but, she is a woman of the streets! I cannot explain it to you, but I am in love with her! God has placed a love in my heart for this woman unlike anything I have ever felt!"

His friend stood there gazing at him while scratching his head, trying to let what he had heard sink in. "A woman of the streets?" He asked. Then he began to plead with Hosea, his words filled with warning. "Now

Hosea," he said, "you know the people will not treat you with kindness. You have spoken so fervently against adultery, and whoredom, but now, you desire to take one of the very flocks of sedition into your own household?"

Hosea knew his friend was one he could trust, and that his words poured out only of concern for him. Hosea turned to face his dear friend while holding a bundle of sticks in his hands. "I know all these things, and I have followed closely after God these many years. But it is God who put her into my heart and it is that same God who is calling me to love her. His love surpasses our understanding; it is Him I must please."

His friend positioned his hands on his hips in complete dismay. "I would argue with you more and try to persuade you to forsake this foolish idea if I thought it would do any good. But I have known you many years and that if you believe something strong enough there is no talking you out of it."

Hosea set the sticks down and looked out as though seeing all of Jerusalem. "My friend, I am sure many people will despise me and hate me. Many will call me a foolish man. But I am counting on you to stand with me and to defend my cause. You know my heart, that I would never do this, if I wasn't sure it was God's perfect will."

His friend gave a sigh of surrender, "then I shall be your confidant," he promised. "If it be God who commands you, we will trust him together. I will be your benefactor!" Both men embraced, sealing the agreement between them.

When Gomer awoke, Hosea had the morning meal
prepared in the courtyard. The aroma drifted inside
through the tiny windows and awoke her senses. As she
descended the threshold, Hosea caught sight of her,
standing in the doorway leaning against the side post. He
was taken aback by her beauty.

"Good morning, oh wonderful donkey trainer," he
said with a smile. "Good morning my grand deliverer,"
Gomer teased. She wandered from the doorway over to
the beast of burden still tied in his place. She gently ran
her fingers down the side of the donkey's neck, as Hosea
looked on. "And just how do you expect a woman to sleep
with the smell of food cooking on the fire?" she asked. "It
wasn't meant to keep you sleeping, but to bring you forth,
that you might sit with me and share bread. Come, it is
now ready," Hosea bid.

Gomer came over and sat down across from him at
the table in the courtyard. Hosea reached across and took
her hand. "What are you doing?" She asked looking in
bewildered fashion. "We shall offer thanksgiving for the
bread," he said. Gomer sat there, eyes wide open staring at
him as he prayed. When he had finished, she began to eat
like she had not taken bread in many days. Hosea sat
amazed at how quickly she devoured every last morsel set
before her.

"I am glad you are here" he said, looking across at
her. "Many days I have thought of you and dreamed of you
being here with me, safe and cared for."

Gomer rose from her position at the table and
walked around the courtyard as though she were

exploring every inch of the place. Hosea watched her every step. The tarnished white garment she wore came down just below her knees. She was barefooted, and her legs were long and laced with strength. Hosea looked away out of embarrassment as she spoke. "I must say the times have been few that men have served me. For as long as I can remember, it has been I who served. I am not sure just how I should respond to this kindness of yours. Are you sure you are not just trying to gain favor with me to also use me like every man I have ever known?"

Hosea arose and started cleaning up the meal, "I have no plans to use you, and in fact you may stay here as long as you wish, for God has put you in my heart. I will care for you and provide for your every need." Gomer now returned to her position of defense as she continued to explore the courtyard, unashamed of her forwardness. "And what may I ask causes you to believe that I would even wish to remain here, or that I desire your provision?"

Hosea now allowed the prophet within him to speak with boldness. He set the dishes down and propped his hands on the table while looking up at her. "If you stay, you shall be cared for, if you choose to leave, then you can expect the same life you have always known. The choice is yours." Hosea this time did not take his eyes off her; he kept glaring at her, with boldness and authority, which made him proud of his courage.

Both eyed each other like two old warriors, who had battled for many years, but now had the fortune of becoming friends. After what seemed like an eternity, she spoke. "I will stay, but with no promise of how long." She awaited a response that she was sure would have conditions to it.

And so it did. Hosea picked the dishes back up and starting walking toward the wash basin as he spoke. "I will agree to this, but with one requirement." Gomer's eyes widened knowing that there was always something expected by men, and that she would prove Hosea was no different.

She asked with arrogant anticipation, "and what is this one thing that you require?" Hosea gently placed the dishes in the water and then walked over to the beast of burden. "The donkey must go, you may stay, but you must promise that the donkey goes!"

Gomer leaned her head forward looking at him in surprise, she had been defeated and she knew it. So the best thing for her to do was to act as though he had just crushed her very spirit. She went over to the donkey and knelt beside it holding on to one of its legs. "NO!" She cried. "Take me, or anything I own, just please, not the donkey." Hosea shook his head, and threw his hands up in the air, "you are a crazy woman, crazy as all the tales I have heard of you." The prophet had prevailed!

****

"I will give you three shekels," the old man said, as he walked around the donkey to examine it. Gomer lit in on him without mercy. "Three shekels? Why, I could get more than that for him if he were blind." Hosea walked in between Gomer and the merchant, taking control of the situation. "We will take it and thank you kind sir for your generous offer," he said while handing the old man the bridle. Hosea watched as the old man counted out three shekels with trembling hands. He gave them to Hosea who in turn presented them to Gomer, and started to walk away. She trailed in behind him making sure that he knew of her displeasure in the price.

Back at the house, Gomer was still ranting over the price of the donkey as Hosea went inside. He soon appeared with a small jar, filled with coins. "Here is the rest of your payment for the donkey," he said, reaching it out to her. Once again, Gomer was left astonished at this man who had come into her life. Never before had she known a man to be so caring and thoughtful.

She was also astonished at how fast coins from a jar could be spent on new clothes, and other items of beauty. Something she had never been able to do before. Over the coming days she explored every shop and back alley in Jerusalem. She lavished herself with beautiful fabric and silk garments.

One evening upon returning from her extravaganza of buying, she entered the courtyard, and called out to Hosea to come see her glamorous purchases. But he did not answer! She was surprised at the feeling of concern that arose within her. It was the first sign in her own heart that she was beginning to care for this man.

"Hosea, Hosea!" she called out over and over, as she searched throughout the house. Finally from the top of the staircase leading up to the roof he answered. "I am up here, just been putting some things together," he said.

Gomer stood at the bottom of the steps looking up at him, furious at him for frightening her so. He descended the stairs and came down to her. "Now, now, tonight is not a time for anger," he said walking around behind her. "This is a night of happiness, and joy." He retrieved a small piece of cloth from her newly purchased items and carefully tied it around her eyes. "What are you doing, you crazy prophet?" She asked playfully. Hosea said nothing; he just ever so gently began to lead her up the stairs. Both of them laughed at her awkwardness of trying to ascend the steps without the ability to see.

"Watch your head," Hosea instructed. She could feel the brush of silk against her arm as she moved through what seemed like a doorway of fabric. He sat her down in a chair, and by the touch of her hand she could tell there was a table set in front of her.

"Alright, you may remove the cloth covering your eyes," Hosea said. Slowly she took it off, and beheld the most beautiful meal set before her that her eyes had ever seen. The table was filled with fruits and breads, meats and drink. Hosea had masterfully placed oil lamps on short columns sitting to the left and right of the table. Their light cast a soft glow to the surroundings.

Flowers were scattered around the floor and over the table as well. The fabric she had felt brush her arm was that of a silk canopy that covered their hideaway. She blinked with astonishment, "This is the most beautiful thing I have ever seen in all my life," Gomer said half laughing and half wishing to cry at the same time.

The evening was spent with both journeying from their separate worlds to find a common ground between them. As strange as it may seem, they began to realize that it was their great differences that actually drew them closer. It was more of an enchantment of interest, each intrigued with one another, and the opposite worlds from which they came. The night ended with Gomer softly kissing Hosea on the cheek. "Good night my grand deliverer," she romantically whispered and descended the stairs to prepare for sleep.

The next few weeks were filled with both joy and trial as they became better acquainted. Hosea learned to adjust to her fits of rage. And Gomer learned to tolerate his lifestyle of a prophet. But one thing was sure, Hosea was gently and gradually disarming Gomer's distrust, and causing her to appreciate the abundant life now being provided for her.

Every night Hosea would stay at his friend's home allowing Gomer to have full access to his own house. His friend, wise and gentle always seemed to know the right words, to encourage him. Many nights they sat long on the roof of his friend's home with Hosea pouring his heart out, freely and without judgment. It was the kind of friendship that allowed for perfect honesty between these two men.

They discussed the deep spiritual questions of life, but never inquired of one another anything deeper than what each openly shared on their own. It was an unspoken rule between them. There was one unanswered question that burned within Hosea's heart about his friend that was never answered. And Hosea, out of respect for his friend, would never have asked. Where did his

friend go to for long periods at a time? For his friend
simply would leave for weeks at a time, but never offered
any explanation. Hosea simply did not press the issue.

Before Hosea and Gomer knew it days had turned
into weeks, and weeks into months, and animosity, into
love. They spent every waking moment together! Hosea
would rise early and plan some journey for the day,
something exciting and adventurous. They traveled to
nearby villages like Bethlehem to explore more shops and
sights. They always arrived home in time for both to go
their separate ways, Gomer to Hosea's house and Hosea to
the home of his friend.

It was in those days that Hosea began to consider
taking her to be his wife. But many things lay heavy on his
mind! Because he knew she was not a virgin, and in fact
had been with many men, all the sinful stains, from each
ungodly act would be laid upon him. Was he willing to
bear the burden of her past to give her a glorious future?

After many days of prayer and thought concerning
this matter Hosea finally yielded himself to the will of
God. One day he journeyed with Gomer out of Jerusalem,
and down the road leading toward Bethlehem. They were
enveloped with beautiful fields spread out in front of
them. Long haired sheep grazed upon the hills and
flowers in colors of purple and yellow filled the
countryside.

He led her beside a small brook, gently rolling
through the hills and when he had found the perfect place
he carefully spread out a blanket for them to sit upon. The

warm breeze lifted her black hair as it teasingly played with it. Hosea took her by the hand.

"Gomer, I have brought you here today in this beautiful place to ask you to be my wife. Have I not shown my love for you, have I not spoken of how my very heart aches for you to be mine?"

Gomer reached over and gently wiped a tear from his face as it flowed softly down his cheek. "Hosea you are a good man, your heart is as pure as these mountain streams, and you have given me more joy in these last days, than I have known in all my life. But we are so different. I am not sure that I could live by your righteous ways. My past is like a garment I will carry with me always and one that I cannot remove. It is the only life I have known. I have prayed a million prayers to change; to mend my ways and to know how it feels to truly love someone."

Gomer paused and reflected for a moment on just how her life had changed over the last few months. Her eyes moistened as she could no longer resist the love which had grown in her heart for Hosea. She leaned over and delicately kissed his lips.

The taste of their kiss was still on her lips when she said; "oh, Hosea, I have grown to love you, I know I have! And my love for you tears at me, ripping my very heart in pieces." She took both of his hands into her own; "Is your love for me strong enough, oh my grand deliverer, to abide patiently with me, even if I should waver from the path of righteousness?"

Hosea thought long and hard before answering. "Gomer, my love for you is without condition! I will love you always, and I will make a covenant with you this day that I will forever remain faithful unto you. Let my very soul waste away, before I should forsake you!"

Gomer leaned over and kissed his lips once more, and then taking a sip of wine from a cup set before her, she sealed the covenant between them.

Chapter 7

Miracles Do Come in the Middle of the Night

"Before I fashioned you in your mother's womb I was acquainted with everything about you, and before you were born, I consecrated you unto myself..."

Jeremiah 1:5

Hosea felt the hand of Gomer shaking him, attempting to awake him. "Hosea, Hosea, wake up, the baby is coming." He sat up getting his senses about him and then realizing what had just been said. "What, the baby, it's time for the baby!" Gomer tried to stay calm as she encouraged him, "Yes Hosea, you must go quickly and fetch the midwife."

He leaped upright and raced as quickly as his legs could carry him through the darkened streets to fetch Naomi the midwife. She had delivered more babies in this community than anyone could ever take count of. Naomi entered the doorway of the house with the usual greeting of warmth and delight that seemed to abide with her wherever she went. "Oh, we are going to have a baby!" she said. "Miracles do come in the middle of the night, now don't they?"

Pleasant smiles and kind words attended her every deed, even if it was long into the night. She immediately set about giving orders to Hosea. "Now fix us a fire in the courtyard and put some water to boiling, bring us some fabric and plenty of soft matting for Gomer to lie upon." Hosea arranged all these things as quickly as he could, and then moved to the side and watched the two women converse. He walked over and knelt down by Gomer. "Tonight, God shall bring us a gift from your very body, and thereby He shall bless many people. I love you my dear Gomer." He leaned down and kissed her forehead tenderly.

"That man makes over me way too much," Gomer said. Naomi patted her face with the warmth of the wet cloth. "Hush now child, don't go using your strength to brag about that man of yours, you will need all that breath for delivering this baby."

Hosea walked next door to the house of his friend. He was already up, awakened with the commotion of fire building and talk of a baby coming. Hosea went up on the roof to join his friend. The coolness of the night air sent a chill over them as they took up their positions of waiting.

"Well I certainly never expected to see this day come," his friend exclaimed, "the day when the prophet Hosea would become a father." "Neither did I my good friend, neither did I," Hosea said, while finding a seat facing the courtyard of his own home.

The two men sat for many hours and conversed about how life would soon change for Hosea. "You will be a wonderful father," his friend encouraged, "you have more patience than any man I have ever known." Hosea looked over at his friend, who by now had his feet propped up on the ledge surrounding the top of his house. "I am very thankful to have you here with me at this special moment," Hosea responded.

A few times Hosea's eyes would grow heavy as the wait became long; the words exchanged between them becoming slower and fewer as they spoke. The night sky above them was lit by a million stars and the cold air caused every breath they took to rise with a heavy mist. Hosea lifted his head and watched as a soft cloud passed in front of the fully lit moon. He silently prayed for Gomer, and Naomi, asking God for a child that would honor the Lord, and bring blessings upon their household.

From the windows of their home came the sound of Gomer in great travail. Hosea listened compassionately but was unable to bring ease to the screams, and cries of childbirth. He was lost in deep concern for Gomer, and hadn't noticed that his friend had slipped away for a few moments. He was startled as his friend reappeared with some hot tea and set it before him. Hosea reached for the soothing brew. "If I could but take her place, and bear her pain, I would you know?" His friend took up his position once again, "yes I believe you would take her place Hosea, but the prophet has not the power to heal her pain."

Hosea sipped the tea, its warmth filling his insides, and providing resistance against the night chill. The friend handed Hosea a blanket to cover up with and also recovered himself while he asked; "is there a name within your heart for this child?" Hosea shook his head thoughtfully from side to side, "I have been praying and asking God to bring a name into my heart that would please Him but until this very moment I haven't a name."

His friend spoke to him plainly and with great love. "I have lived by you for many years, and never have I known a man with a more pure heart than you Hosea. I know that in our custom the child would normally be named after the father or mother, or perhaps someone in your lineage. But because your spirit seeks the will of God, you will obey him and walk after the counsel of His voice."

After what seemed like many hours Hosea suddenly sat upright, listening carefully to hear the blessed sound of a baby crying. He slowly stood and smiled while tears began to stream down his face.

Walking but a few steps to the edge of his friend's roof, he was able to peer down upon the courtyard of his own home. He watched the doorway with nervous anticipation for Naomi to appear. The strong heavy hand of his friend gently came down upon his shoulder. "Soon we shall know if God has brought honor upon your household, with the birth of a son." Hosea raised his hand and placed it on top of his friend's hand. "Let the sovereign will of God be done, for I have given my heart to trust him," he responded.

Soon Naomi appeared in the doorway and quietly called out to Hosea. He descended the steps with an unexpected feeling of apprehension. The few short steps from the house of his friend now seemed long, and frightening. Feeling displaced, like a guest in his own home, his hand pushed back the curtain entrance leading into where Gomer and their newborn baby lay.

Gomer lay there holding on her chest a child wrapped tight in white cloth. "Hosea," she said, eyes beaming with pride, "God has given us a son." He knelt beside her and tenderly placed his large hand on the top of the baby's head, softly caressing the dark black hair. Hosea began to pray, "God you have blessed us this night with a gift from heaven, and to you oh Lord is thanksgiving now and for evermore."

In his heart Hosea felt as though he was looking upon a miracle. He stayed by Gomer's side for a long time, and became so deep in thought that he forgot about Naomi, who was cleaning up the vessels. It was her words that brought him back to full consciousness. "Tomorrow we will need some salt and more cloth for the purity wrapping."

Hosea quietly acknowledged her orders, "yes Naomi, tomorrow I will fetch some from the market." But Naomi just continued to move around the room, like a shadow's silent presence. Hosea sat looking upon his wife and new born son, filled with pride and joy. He watched as Naomi ministered to Gomer, carefully assisting her and ministering to her every need. "Naomi," he said, "you are

an angel sent from God; may the Lord bless you always."
After a while all motion within the room began to cease,
as weariness fell upon them all. Hosea drifted from
consciousness into sleep, believing that tomorrow many
would celebrate with him the birth of their firstborn son.

Hosea awoke still sitting in the chair with a
covering over him for warmth. Adjusting his eyes to the
first morning light he pondered that Naomi must surely
have placed the covering over him after he had fallen
asleep. Gently he eased from the chair so as to not make
any noise, and softly walked over to where Gomer lay
with their baby close to her side.

"*You're the most beautiful woman in the entire world*" he
thought to himself. From the first night of their encounter
until now, Hosea had seen such change in her. He wanted
so to reach down in the quietness of the morning dawn
and at least kiss her cheek, but he dare not for fear of
waking her. He quietly walked outside into the courtyard
and found Naomi sitting by the fire oven for warmth. The
light of morning was just beginning to rise over the
eastern mountains. It cast a painted sky of orange and
reds. The atmosphere was quiet, and peaceful; Hosea had
never felt more alive and fulfilled in all his life.

When Naomi saw Hosea emerge from the house,
almost immediately she began to instruct Him. "You go on
now into the market place and fetch those things we need
and I will stay here and tend to Gomer. When you arrive
back, I will have the morning meal prepared for you."

But before Hosea could turn to leave, Naomi then
took him captive by the look of concern on her face.

"Hosea," she said now speaking to him as though she were his own mother. "I know you are overjoyed with the birth of your son, but please Hosea, don't allow your heart to grow weary by the judgment of what others might say or think about this child."

Hosea stood frozen in thought. Without warning the ambience of the morning had been snapped away as He felt a deep sense of apprehension flood his soul. "Has there been talk within the community, something that I am not aware of?" He asked.

Naomi leaned forward, and with her wrinkled hands from many years of labor, picked up a rod. She poked at the fire, as though she would not even answer him, as sparks ascended up into the morning sky. "Do you see those sparks going up into the heavens?" She asked.

Hosea watched them fly upwards until they melted away. Naomi continued, "One of those sparks can set a whole city ablaze, just one mind you. So can talk Hosea, so can talk! People can be cruel, without mercy. All I am saying is that it would be wise for you to prepare your heart if men do not speak so kindly to you concerning this child, and his mother Gomer. God may forgive us our sins, but man's judgment can pierce through to the very soul."

Hosea had already pondered these things but had simply tucked them away, choosing rather to believe that he would not be faced with such harsh criticism. "Thank you for your words of wise counsel Naomi, I shall guard my heart, that I might not grow weary. I shall endure whatever pain is laid upon me, for the joy of knowing and obeying the will of God will sustain me."

Hosea started walking through the city, into the area of merchants. In his heart he pondered and considered the words spoken to him by Naomi. With each step, he built a defensive wall against any words of judgment that might come to him. As a prophet he had many times endured the harsh and thoughtless expectations of others. But this was different now! It was one thing if someone lashed out at him, but it was yet another for someone to cast judgment upon an innocent child. A holy anger arose within him and cast a hedge about him. "This is bone of my bone and flesh of my flesh," he said out loud to himself.

Soon he was standing inside the shop filled with fabrics and woven wools. Hosea placed his hands on the table of the shop keeper, and leaned forward on the support of his strong arms. "I wish to purchase swaddling cloth, enough for the days of purification of a child." The shop keeper lifted his head to greet the first customer of the day.

The merchant was short and round, wearing a long flowing garment white as pure salt itself. His hair neatly combed, and his cheeks filled with rose colored red. He was the picture of *hesed*, the friendliness that every Jew desires to render. "Well this is a blessed start to the morning. And tell me sir is this child your own?" He asked.

Hosea's heart now beat with more ease, "Yes sir, the child is mine, born just this morning, a male of the House of Israel." The keeper now extended his hand in greeting, "God has shown forth his glory upon thee, my brother, my heart rejoices with you." They embraced across the table, as the room became filled with laughter and joyous celebration.

"Let's see what we can find here, it must be the very best for an occasion such as this," the keeper said. He hurriedly turned and began to dig through piles of cloth and mumbling to himself all the while. Hosea looked on, his spirit soaring within him at the reception given him by the shop keeper. Finally his new found benefactor returned carrying in his arms the cloth wrappings for purification. He laid it on the table, then examined it one last time as though making sure it was fit to be placed upon the body of one so pure. "I believe this will serve you well, my friend." he said with confidence. "And what shall be the price?" Hosea asked looking down into his money bag for coins with which to pay.

"For you it is a gift; a blessing in honor of what God has done unto you." Both men embraced again, and Hosea was overwhelmed with great joy. "Thank you, shalom and blessing from the Lord unto you!" he said.

Then the shop keeper asked, "What is your name that I may tell others of this wonderful blessing that God has brought to our city today." A rush of apprehension now flowed into the room like a mighty wave from the sea. "My name is Hosea, the Prophet, and my wife is Gomer, we live..." but before he could finish speaking the eyes of the keeper had widened. His face was now pale, showing disbelief that perhaps he was contributing to some sinful act. He began pushing Hosea toward the doorway of his market. "Take your cloth and be gone! And say nothing of this to anyone, that I have provided you fabric wherewith to cover this child. For I have heard of you and your wife of whoredoms, and I but plead God's mercies upon you," the keeper said forcefully. Hosea started to speak in defense of Gomer and his child, but instead, the hand of the keeper was raised in defiance of any explanation.

Hosea walked the road back to his house, with all the heaviness his very soul could bear. "God what are you doing?" he asked, "I don't understand why my son has to bear this, there is no sin in him, not one word of guile has been uttered from his sweet lips, but he is already being condemned."

Every step became heavy, his feet felt like bricks of mortar, pulling at his very soul dragging it down into grief. Finally he could not bear his sorrow any longer. He left the pathway and found a place of solitude, and falling upon the ground he began to weep. His tears stained the very cloth he would use to wrap his precious son in. He could speak no words, for they could not express his pain. His lips moved quietly, speaking from the depth of his heart and soul. Without warning the air begin to stir around his place of sorrow. Hosea felt what he thought to be a giant hand touch his shoulder. He jumped in surprise and quickly turned to face whoever might be near him. But there was no one to be seen! Only the feeling of strength and courage could be felt as it flooded his soul. "God has surely laid His hand upon me," he said out loud. His angels encamp around those who fear Him!" He began to lift his hands in praise and adoration of God's abiding presence.

As he entered the courtyard he saw Naomi, setting a place for them to take bread. She quickly motioned for him to keep silence, "Shhhh," she whispered, "You must come and hear the beauty that pours out from your household." She carefully led him inside, safely behind the curtain where Gomer and the child lay. He stood listening to the most beautiful lullaby being sung by Gomer that his ears had ever heard.

"Sweet little baby don't you cry
In my arms you safely lie

A gift from God you must be
Brought from heaven down to me

I promise you to do my best
To bring you joy and happiness

Till all my days on earth are done
And we shall rest at set of sun."

Hosea stood listening, his heart filled with such pride for his wife. But also his heart ached inside. *"If they only knew, if the people could only open their hearts and know the change that has taken place within the heart of Gomer, then they would find mercy for her and our child,"* he thought.

The next days were filled with ministry to Gomer and the child. Hosea moved about caring for his family, both with joy and yet a cloud of heaviness covering his spirit. He knew that he would have a great responsibility to protect his household from the slanderous words already being spoken by the community.

On the sixth day after the child's birth, Hosea returned home after a day of preaching by the Yarmulke River. Gomer was busy wrapping the child and washing him with the salt for purification. When she saw Hosea approach, she quickly ran to greet him. Throwing her arms around him she was filled with excitement; her face glowing with radiance. She took his hands in her own and led him to the house. "I know what I desire for the baby's name to be," she said. Hosea was thrilled with her enthusiasm. "Tell me what name you desire!" He said.

Gomer couldn't wait another second, "Joshua!" She exclaimed! "It means deliverer; we will name him after you my wonderful Hosea." With this she threw her arms about the neck of her husband, as though she knew there would be no quarrel with her advice. She stepped back laying her hand on Hosea's chest. "It will forever cast light upon you, my grand deliverer." Her face beamed with pride at her accomplishment as she looked into the face of her husband.

Hosea lowered his head thoughtfully considering her words. "Gomer, nothing could please me more than this! However, my heart is set to obey God. I have prayed fervently unto him that he might place within my heart a name after his choosing. And, if it be that he is pleased with your suggestion, then let it be so!"

Gomer, disappointed that her advice had not met with unwavering approval, ripped her hands away from him. She turned from Hosea and quickly rushed into the house calling out to him all the while. "Well you and God decide then, and I shall but wait to know the name of my own son." Her words were filled with anger toward Hosea. "I am sorry" he yelled back, "I did not mean to hurt you." All the commotion had upset the baby and he started to cry. Hosea walked over and took the baby up in his arms. "Now don't you go fretting little one, we will find a name for you!"

Hosea sat long in the courtyard with the baby held lovingly in his arms. When the evening shadows began to fall, Gomer came out to him. Her spirit now surrendered. She came and sat with them, "I do trust you" she said, "it is just that sometimes I feel my every breath is governed by your righteousness, and that before I can take even a step, some prayer must be offered to gain direction." She reached over and took Hosea's hand, "I am trying desperately to trust you my husband," she said in a spirit of submission.

Hosea and Gomer rose early on the eighth day following the birth of their son. It would be a day of solemn ritual for them, the day of naming him, and of circumcision for their son.

"So what do you think?" Gomer asked. Hosea looked up to see her standing before him holding the child. He was dressed in a hand woven garment, in colors of blue and white. "I made it for him myself," Gomer said, standing there elated with pride. Hosea came over and laid his hand upon him. "I think it is a garment fit for a king, it will serve him well."

At the Temple complex they found the place where they might present him unto the Lord. Gomer looked around in bewildered astonishment at the beautiful buildings of the Temple. "Come on," Hosea encouraged, "you act like this is your first time to ever be in the Temple precinct", he said. Gomer continued to gaze at the massive pillars lining the portico's as she spoke; "It *is* my first time being here, have you so quickly forgotten who I was before you rescued me?"

As they entered the area delegated for circumcision they were greeted with warmth from the priesthood. One of the priests led them a few steps more into the room of presentation. They found the room to be clean and made of beautiful white stones. Everything about it spoke of holiness and righteousness. Incense burned and filled the room with a sweet odor, and the lamps burned, casting a reflecting light off the polished stones serving both the walls and flooring.

When the priest ordained to perform the circumcision arrived, he introduced himself. "Shalom unto you, my name is Raphael, priest of the covenant of circumcision." He was a man of elder years, tall and lean. His hands showed smoothness and his fingers were long and narrow. Immediately he set about arranging the tools and utensils that would be used in the cutting of flesh. Hosea and Gomer watched the priest as he worked and moved about. His movement was graceful and there was a song that poured forth from his lips. It seemed that every movement was set in time with the rise and fall of the melody. His body swayed and flowed about the room like he was floating on air. When all was made ready, he outstretched his arms toward Hosea and Gomer. "Is it your desire to present this child unto the Lord, to yield him wholly; his body, mind and spirit for the service of the Lord?"

Hosea stepped forward slowly with the child in his arms. "Yes it is our desire to give him unto to the Lord, to be used for His holy purposes." He gently placed the child into the arms of Raphael, who held the baby tight against his chest and began the blessing.

"Blessed are You, Lord our God, King of the universe, who has sanctified us with His commandments and commanded us concerning circumcision."

The baby squirmed and twisted in the priest's hands as he lifting him heavenward. It was one of those moments in life when your mind, without telling it too, captures the image; and you know that for the rest of your life you will never forget the scene. In that moment you could almost have felt the very hands of God reach through the roof and accept the child from the hands of the priest.

Raphael carefully laid the baby on a table of pure marble. It was polished so clean that it seemed no other child had ever lain there before. He carefully uncovered the baby, and the child gave a small whimper as his arms and legs stretched out, immediately responding to being freed.

As the cutting of flesh took place, Hosea's heart rejoiced at the mighty work of God, and the fulfillment of all the days that had led them here. His mind raced back to the first encounter with Gomer, then to the calling of God to take her to be his wife, and now standing here in this place was the culmination of a willingness to obey God's voice.

Hosea felt a hand slip into his; it was that of Gomer, and the hand was soft like the petals of a rose. When he turned to look into her eyes, she was crying. Tears were flowing down both of her ivory cheeks. A smile passed between them, and she leaned over to whisper something into his ear. "Hosea, I love you, I love you with all my heart, and whatsoever name God has put in your heart for this child, so let it be. You are my husband, and my heart is with you." Hosea felt the weight of worry lift from his shoulders. He leaned to her and gently kissed her lips, the taste of joyous tears were upon them!

The cry of pain filled the room as the covenant of circumcision was fulfilled. A child was brought into fellowship with the Household of Israel.

Raphael instructed Hosea to place his hands on the baby's head and proclaim a name for the child, a name that all heaven and earth would bear witness to. Gomer gave one last grip of affirmation and then released Hosea's hand, as she watched her husband walk to the table and gently place his hands on the head of their child.

Hosea looked up toward the heavens. "God, who is rich in mercy, has brought into my heart a name. While I was in prayer just yesterday, through revelation by The Holy Spirit, He instructed me that the child's name shall be, Jezreel." Hosea continued, "For this child shall be a seed of the Lord, planted to bring forth victory, and to bruise the head of the enemy." When he had finished he cast his eyes toward Gomer, desiring to find accord between them. Gomer's face glowed with approval!

Raphael cradled Jezreel up into his arms and began to pray,

"Creator of all things; may it be Thy gracious will to regard and accept this covenant, as if I had brought this baby before Thy glorious throne. And Thou, in Thy abundant mercy, through Thy holy angels, give a pure and holy heart to Jezreel, the son of his father Hosea, and his mother Gomer. This child whose name is Jezreel was circumcised in honor of Thy great Name. May his heart be wise in understanding Thy Holy Law! And cause him to learn Your ways oh LORD and teach others thy law. May Jezreel always keep and fulfill thy precepts, AMEN!"

Chapter 8

God Knows What We Need, Before Each Day Begins

"Your God will supply everything you have need of, through the abundant riches of His glory in Christ Jesus."

Philippians 4:19

Many days had passed since the death of their dear friend Shekina. Jezreel had returned to meeting with the priests each day and sharing the story of his father and mother. As the days wore on and many questions were answered, Jezreel became more convinced he was doing the right thing.

On one particular day when the air within the chamber grew heavy from the heat of the late afternoon sun, Malchiah laid his hand upon Jezreel's shoulder, "You may conclude your narrative for today, go my son and take rest," he said. Jezreel sighed relief as the beads of sweat began to form on his brow. "Thank you my lord, I have spoken with you from my heart as God hath lead me." Malchiah walked with him to the doorway and instructed Zadok to show him to their chamber.

As the two men walked together, Jezreel began to question him. "What news comes to you concerning the welfare of our community and of our home? Do you think when I have concluded my chronicle with you about my father and mother that we shall be able to return to our home?"

Zadok's steps ceased and he motioned for Jezreel to follow him. They walked across the complex to the southern end of the stone pavement. The platform gave them a lofty view of much of the city. In the distance Jezreel could see the hillside of the Makhtesh where they had lived.

"Jezreel," Zadok began, "your home is no more; the men that took the life of your friend have also broken down the very walls of your house. If they could get to you, they would take your life as well." Jezreel felt as though the very air from within him had been violently drawn from his body. "What will we do, where shall we abide, I have a family, and I must provide a place for them?"

Zadok invited him to sit down upon a stone bench which provided rest to visitors at the Temple. Just the atmosphere of the place brought some peace to his soul. Tall cedars grew from small garden squares in between the flooring stones, and their leaves gently rustled and swayed in the afternoon breeze. Zadok joined him on the bench, and talked as friend to friend.

"Jezreel, God in his wisdom always foresees our path, and he knows what we shall need, even before each day begins. Do you believe this?" He asked. Jezreel's mind quickly attempted to look into the heart of Zadok. Did he know something that he was not fully telling him? Had there already been some provision made that Zadok had not told him of? Should he press him further to understand?

Finally Jezreel stood and walked away from Zadok who was still sitting on the bench. Jezreel spoke over his shoulder while he studied the sprawling ant like city below. "Yes I do believe these things, and I will once again commit myself to trust only but the Lord my provider. It is he that made the heavens, and the earth belongs to him also."

Zadok approached, and stood with him, both men looking in the direction of where Jezreel's home had been. "Jezreel," he said, "before you were even born God was providing for this day, and even now has made a place for you. Just have faith and you will understand all my words later on."

Zadok turned to walk away, ready to lead him back to their chamber. But Jezreel just stood there! "May I stay here and have some time to myself a while, that I might pray and consider these things? And after you have given me some time, would you bring my wife and son here to me in this place?"

The priest bowed his head in resolve. "Yes Jezreel I shall do your bidding! All I ask is that you do not depart from this place for your safety and for your well being." "I shall stay," Jezreel said, and then Zadok turned and was gone.

By the time Zadok brought Mishi and Anna, the sun was slowly beginning its descent behind the city walls to the west. As Mishi caught sight of his dear Abba, he quickly ran ahead of his mother and Zadok to greet him. It always felt good to have his Abba's arms wrapped tight around him. He buried his face into Jezreel's garment and held on to him, allowing the sweet smell of incense that now hung to the fabric of his clothes, to fill his senses. Anna joined with them, as Mishi turned to see Zadok, walking the path away from them, leaving them alone as a family.

Jezreel began to share with them all the things concerning their home that Zadok had made known to him. "But the priest tells me that a place has already been prepared for us, and that we shall know after a while more concerning it," he said.

The news, although sad, was not unexpected. Jezreel had already spoken to them, attempting to prepare them that they might not be able to return to their beloved home in the Makhtesh. Still an anger rose within Mishi; a fire of contempt burned within his heart.

Suddenly a strange feeling overcame Mishi. He walked to the edge of the temple courtyard and stood against the wall surrounding the complex. He looked out into the direction of where their home had been, and it was as though he could see himself only a few days ago standing on the roof of their home looking at the Temple where he now stood. Time seemed to reverse itself and played tricks on his mind. The faces of the men from the community came before him, the men that he was sure had been responsible for the destruction of their home. In his heart he searched for a stone, a pebble to cast toward them. When his mind had found one; one as tall as the mountains, he made ready to cast it in their direction. But the man within him grabbed him and would not let him fulfill his wish. Slowly, in his mind, he laid the stone back down. "I am better than that. I will not let their evil destroy my good," he said out loud. He went back to his Abba and momma, filled with strength and pride in himself. Pride, that he had conquered his anger, and hatred.

When the evening grew dark they made their way back to their new home. Mishi had come to full acceptance that he would not call it "our chambers" any more. But until they knew where they would live, he would make this his home, and he would do all he could to take care of Anna while Jezreel was with the priest each day.

As they drew nearer they could tell that many torches burned brightly throughout the complex surrounding the Temple. Many people moved about in rapid pace. When they passed through the gate leading to their home, the priests were rushing throughout the walkways.

One such priest moved past them pushing one of the smaller vessels of the Great Golden Basin. It had been emptied of all its purity water, and its wheels made eerie noises as it passed.

"Is there something of which we should be concerned?" Jezreel asked, as the priest moved beyond them. He did not respond to Jezreel's question, he just kept moving forward. Soon another passed them, carrying two arks bearing scrolls, one in each arm. Mishi looked at the priest feet and watched them, swiftly moving him along over the rocks, his long white robe whipping about in the night air. Finally they came to the doorway of their home, and moved inside as quickly as they could.

"Jezreel, what could be happening?" Anna asked. Her voice had uneasiness about it, which made little Mishi's insides quake, as when the earth trembles.

The sounds of continual movement outside their door caused him to keep his eyes upon it. Mishi became their self-appointed watchman. Jezreel went about laying out the bed mats, and Anna offered Mishi some bread and honey. He took small pieces and then gently dipped it into the honey and slowly raised it to his mouth, keeping a constant vigil on the doorway of their refuge. The light from night torches would occasionally leap inside through the cracks of the door for a brief moment whiles those moving outside walked by.

After many hours of dutiful watch on the door, Mishi's eyes grew weary. "Abba", he called out, "may I lay with you and momma tonight?" "Yes, Mishi come and lay with us," Jezreel invited. His Abba's arms drew tight around him, as he lay with his back against Jezreel. Mishi was still turned toward the doorway and watched every flicker of light which passed by. It wasn't long before he was fast asleep.

His haven of rest was disturbed by voices. It was the voice of Zadok, and of his Abba. Mishi had heard no knock, nor the opening of the door. He felt he had failed in his mission as watchman!

Mishi slowly positioned himself up on the mat, and in the dimness of the light from Zadok's lantern, he could tell that Anna was standing with them also. Her hands were placed on her hips, and she was just listening. "Abba," he said with his arms held up toward him, "What is happening?" Jezreel reached down and picked him up. Mishi's bare legs clung to him as tightly as they could. Although he held Mishi, Jezreel's attention was with Zadok.

"...Then we shall come with you," he heard his Abba say to Zadok. Anna began immediately to gather a few belongings for the journey, wherever that might be, but the priest interrupted her. "You have no time for gathering anything; just follow me!" Zadok spoke, with authority and much persuasion.

When they stepped outside the doorway, Mishi was surprised to see other priests still busily moving objects, their white robes making them more visible in the night. "Abba, let me walk," he said, "I am much too big for you to carry."

The flooring stones were cold to his bare feet, as Jezreel sat him down. "What is the hour?" He heard his Abba ask. "It is the last of the middle watch." Zadok responded. From this they knew that in a few more hours and it would be the light of day.

As they followed Zadok down the walkway, Mishi felt like he could feel the breath of the men from the community breathing heavy upon him. His mind had concluded that they were coming, and would attempt to overthrow the priesthood. Little did he know however, that a hand far mightier than a few zealots was set to strike against the whole of Jerusalem!

Their pace hastened as they turned down a long hallway, leading north in behind the main Temple House. They went into a small building, and quickly descended many steps leading down under the platform on which the Temple sat. At the bottom of the stairway they moved into a large open room, and Mishi noticed that the air had the smell of being in a cave.

Zadok walked to the western side wall, and drew from under his garment a pouch, and from it he retrieved a thin piece of metal. Mishi stood looking up at him, never taking his eyes off the priest. Zadok looked down at him and smiled, he knew his secrets were safe with Mishi.

Moving a stool from the opposite side of the room, he stood upon it, and took the thin piece of metal and slid it into a slit in the rock. He got off the stool, and motioned for them to move away. "Just you watch this," Zadok said looking down at Mishi.

Suddenly the huge rock began to open, turning like it was set with a rod in the middle from floor to ceiling. When the stone had completely opened, Zadok lead them past, where they found another priest on the other side. When they were clear, Zadok and the other priest simply pushed the stone on one side making it turn on its axis until it had positioned itself back in place, with hardly a crack visible in the wall.

The assisting priest handed Zadok back the thin piece of metal with which he quickly deposited back into the pouch under his garment. The excitement of this adventure had caused Mishi to forget all his fear. "How did you do that?" He asked excitedly.

Zadok led him over to the rock door and showed him a lower slit in the stone. "When I placed the metal in the slit high in the rock on the other side, it slid down through a narrow cut in the rock and came out here. The priest then knew it was I, and he let us in," he said. Zadok looked at Mishi and winked, as though he had just entrusted the mystery of the universe over to a child.

They were led down a long hallway, and on either side were many chambers. Most had the doorways opened, and as they passed they could see other priests in some of the rooms. Many were sitting at tables conversing; others were busily arranging objects that perhaps were brought from the Temple and its adjoining buildings. At the end of the hallway, they turned right and entered a room with many people in it.

"This is where you must stay until the siege is over," Zadok said. "There is enough food and water stored here for many months, so you need not worry." The realization that this situation was far worse than he had imagined, began to creep into Mishi's mind. They greeted a few of the people gathered in the room with them and then went over and took a seat against the wall like many others had done. Mishi wiggled his way and sat down between Jezreel's legs. He looked back over his shoulder. "Abba, what does the word *siege* mean, that Zadok spoke of?"

Jezreel turned Mishi around to face him, so that he had his son's full attention. He brushed Mishi's brown hair away from his eyes and began to explain to him what was happening.

"Mishi, the King of Assyria, Sennacherib by name, is coming, and his army is only a day's journey away from the gates of Jerusalem. But we are safe here my son, you need not worry or be afraid, for God has once again foresaw our days, and has brought us here for safe keeping."

While he did not understand all of his Abba's words, he knew enough that it was a dangerous situation. He laid his head on Jezreel's chest to find comfort. His father ran his fingers through his hair, gently caressing it, for he always knew how to make his son feel better.

After some time had passed a priest entered the room. He didn't ask permission to speak he just began to talk as though everyone knew who he was and they were suppose to listen to him. "Brethren, I shall keep you informed of what is happening outside as much as possible. You are all safe here; these chambers are deep under the Temple platform and few from the outside know they are here. There are many supplies here for this very occasion. If you have any questions please feel free to ask, and we will see to it that you are taken care of."

Although they were deep under the temple platform away from the darkness outside, Mishi's body reminded him of the short time he had slept. People were moving about, most of who were either of priestly order, or royal status. You could hear the sound of light whispers from those inside the room. As Mishi's mind drifted he remembered that even while they had been rushed from their home chamber, there was very little noise in doing it. Almost everything except the wheels on the smaller Golden Basin had moved in complete silence. *Was this because of the holiness of the place*, he wondered?

Before he could ponder this question any longer he happened to look up to see an elderly man approaching where they were sitting. He was not of priestly ware Mishi could tell, for the man's garments betrayed him. His clothing was more like that of a prophet, and although filled with many colors, they were faded and humbly worn. The old man used a walking stick to support his aged frame. His face was etched with lines. Many years of worry and toil had cast their handy work. When he got right in front of Mishi he stopped, and stood there looking down upon him.

"Well now just what do we have here, what is your name young man?" He asked, with a raspy voice. Although his voice betrayed the many years which accompanied the gentlemen, the tone with which he spoke demanded respect.

Mishi looked at Anna and Jezreel seeking approval to answer him. "Go ahead, tell him your name son," his father said releasing him to make a new friend. "My name is Mishi sir; I am the son of Jezreel and Anna." He felt pride rise up within himself at the way he had answered.

The old man rubbed the top of Mishi's head. "You certainly are a bright young man of strength and wisdom; perhaps we could find some chore for you while we are down here, one to ease your mind of the happenings of the day." Mishi looked at his Abba and mother once again to receive their approval of such an invitation.

Jezreel rose to his feet and extended his hand, "and what dear sir, is the name of one so kind as to offer my son a grand assignment?" The old man shook Jezreel's hand assuredly, and then placed both his hands on the top of his walking stick so as to support himself. "My name is Isaiah, son of Amoz; I am a prophet of the Lord."

They were all taken back by the realization that one of the mightiest prophets of all Israel was now standing before them. "It is our joy and great pleasure to have your acquaintance," Jezreel responded.

The prophet looked at Mishi and gave a wink of his eye, "Well when you are as old as I am, you are just glad to still be making some acquaintances." They all gave out a modest laugh together. Jezreel asked him, "but why are you here, in the Temple complex, and within these chambers?"

Isaiah walked over to a seat fashioned against the wall and turned to sit down. Their eyes were still cast on him with amazement that he was even there with them. The old prophet attempted to persuade his body to cooperate by slowly easing into the seat. "Well now to answer your question as to why I am here, well, that's where this young man's chores will come in," he said, giving a faint nod in Mishi's direction.

By now he had managed to arrange himself in the seat and took a deep breath as though worn out from the ordeal. "You see when you are forced to sit and listen to an old man tell stories about the events that brought him here, well now that is a chore in and of itself."

Once again quiet laughter poured forth from the small assembly. Mishi went and moved right in front of him so not to miss one word that came from Isaiah's parched lips. His eyes gazed up in astonishment as he looked into the face of one of the greatest prophets in Israel's history. Anna and Jezreel sat with them, just as eager to hear his story.

Mishi gave a soft yawn, as the early morning hours still tried to take him captive. But he determined not to allow himself to slip into its clutches. The prophet set his walking stick in front of him using it as a support, and began his intriguing narrative.

Chapter 9

The Angel of God Walks Over Jerusalem

"Then the angel of the LORD went, and slaughtered in the camp of the Assyrians,
One hundred- eighty five thousand men. And when they arose early in the morning, behold, they were all dead corpses."

Isaiah 37: 36

The prophet Isaiah cleared his voice; "a few days ago, I was brought here at the command of King Hezekiah. He had learned of the impending siege of Sennacherib, King of Assyria. I was brought here to pray, to ask for direction from the Lord God of Israel. I was to seek our God for wisdom concerning this wicked king that has set his heart against Israel, and now to overtake Jerusalem."

Isaiah paused, knowing what he had spoken was enough to cause Mishi's heart to fear greatly. The prophet leaned down so he was eye level with him. "But don't you worry my little friend, for Sennacherib will not accomplish this thing which he has determined to do. For God will resist him!"

Mishi squirmed around in excitement as Isaiah continued. "When the eyes of the Lord saw the evil intention of Sennacherib, He spoke into the heart of King Hezekiah! He moved upon him to set about digging a water tunnel from the Gihon Spring, leading under the city walls, that we might have a vast supply to sustain us. The workmen have now accomplished this task, by the wisdom of Almighty God. And when they were finished, the workmen inscribed an account of their accomplishment on the walls of the tunnel."

Mishi was captivated by the intriguing story, and did not allow Isaiah the time to carry on with his narrative before interrupting him with a question. "Do you know what the writing said that the workmen wrote on the wall in the tunnel?"

Isaiah didn't hesitate, "I certainly do know what it says, and in fact I memorized it. I was taken into the tunnels after the workmen were finished and was shown the writing. As I stood there I memorized every line."

Isaiah looked past his little audience as though he was addressing a mighty assembly.

"While the workman raised the pick each toward his fellow.
And while there remained three cubits to be tunneled through.
There was heard the voice of a man calling to his fellow.
For there was a split in the rock.
On the right hand and on the left hand.
And on the day of the tunneling through the workman struck

each in the direction of his fellow, pick against pick.

And the water started flowing from the source to the pool.
Twelve hundred cubits.
And the height of the rock above the head of the workman
was a hundred cubits."

Isaiah focused his attention back to Jezreel's family once again, "So the reason I am here, is because King Hezekiah sent for me. I have been here many days offering counsel to the king concerning this matter, and that, my new found friends, is why I am here."

When he had finished speaking, Jezreel moved close so as not to allow anyone else to hear. "This tunnel that you speak of, we also have heard of it, and for this cause we are here. Within that tunnel a scroll was found bearing the name of my father Hosea. And I have come to bear witness of the truth concerning my father, and his scribed words."

The prophet's eyes now burned as though they had the very fire of God within them, as he looked upon Jezreel. "My son let nothing turn your heart from proclaiming all that the Lord might bid you. For many souls might find the righteous path because of your words." Jezreel's heart was full of emotions at the encouraging words of the mighty prophet. "Thank you my lord, I will not forget thy words, I will bind them around my heart to give me courage," he said.

Jezreel and the prophet Isaiah talked long into the morning, softly conversing together. Anna had prepared

Mishi a bed from some covers provided in the room. He lay near the wall, facing the little assembly, nice and warm under the thick wool covering. He watched and listened until the words they spoke became muddled in his head. The warmth from his bed called out to his body, ordering it to sleep. Finally his eyes could yield no more resistance, and he surrendered to its demands.

As he slept, soldiers from mighty armies marched through his mind. Men with picks and hammers, chiseled through hard rock. They called to one another, and gave out warnings of water that was rising. One carried a jar in his hand and took from it a scroll, and when they opened it, a light poured forth, filling all the earth. And then he was carried back to their home, their beloved home in the Makhtesh. Oh how he longed for it, just to be there with Shekina once more. Just to go up on the roof and sit in his favorite spot to think or play. Now he dreamed he was running and playing with his friends, while Anna baked bread. He was telling them of the mighty prophet Isaiah, and that he was kind, but spoke with such power and authority.

All through the day his bed mat took him on a journey, flying him quickly from one scene to another, until he safely returned to the secret hideaway.

It was the hunger of his stomach that awoke him late into the afternoon. He arose attempting to determine if his mind was still tricking him or if he was truly awake. He sat up and placed his back against the wall pulling his knees up to rest his arms upon. When Anna saw that he was awake she came over and sat down by him. "I was beginning to think you were going to sleep all day," she said. Mishi laid his head over against her arm feeling the warmth from her skin on his face. "Momma I'm hungry, may I have something to eat?" he asked. "Well let's just see what we can find around here." She took him by the hand lifting him up to his feet. They walked over to a big table filled with all kinds of foods. "Momma where did all this food come from?" His eyes widened with excitement at the sight of the meal set before him. "The priests provided it for us my son, now sit and eat all you wish."

He sat down with his bare legs hanging over the edge of the seat. His chin rose just above the side of the table. Anna moved about the table busily placing meats, breads, and fruits on his dish. His mind had been so consumed with hunger that he had not noticed that his Abba was not present. "Momma where's Abba, and where is the prophet Isaiah?"

Anna continued her movements around the table, arranging and cleaning up where others had eaten, as she spoke to him.

"Mishi, King Hezekiah is now at the Temple, and he has summoned the prophet to come up and speak with him. As Isaiah left he asked your Abba to go with him, to be his companion, and serve as a witness to the words that would be spoken between them."

"Abba is going to meet the King?" Mishi questioned with much excitement. Anna tried to calm him, "Yes Mishi, your Abba is going to meet King Hezekiah. It seems God's favor is shining on us."

After many hours of waiting, Mishi looked up to see Jezreel and the prophet returning to them. Jezreel was assisting Isaiah by holding on to his arm as he walked. The prophet's steps were slow, with each one being taken in great care. Mishi did not wait for them to make the full length of the room. He leaped to his feet and went to meet them about midways. "So did you see the king?" He asked. Anna scolded him from across the room! "Mishi, don't ask too many questions."

The prophet raised his head slightly, to find him in his sight. "Now, just let me sit down, young man and catch my breath, then I will tell you everything that took place during our audience with the king."

Mishi took over Jezreel's position of assisting the prophet, he slipped his hand inside Isaiah's and gently led him the last remaining steps. He kept a constant vigil upon the prophet's feet, looking down at them, hoping his own concern would make every step land with perfection.

When they got to the seat against the wall, the old prophet turned and sat down as though one more step would have taken away his very life breath. "That was just about all I could do. One more step, and I think it would have gotten me," he said. Mishi sat down on the floor in front of him looking up with anticipation to understand what had happened, and to know of their safety. He watched Isaiah's chest rise and fall with each breath, in the hope that the next one would provide enough strength that he might begin his account.

Jezreel had secured a drink for the prophet, and he handed it to him and then sat by Anna. Isaiah's hand shook as he lifted the cup to his lips to refresh himself. He leaned over slightly to one side and set the cup on the stone floor.

Isaiah stabled his breath and searched the eyes of the small gathering. "King Hezekiah is a good man. I trust that his heart fears God and seeks after him. However, when we arrived up at the Temple to have audience with him, he was very afraid. For Sennacherib King of Assyria has surrounded the city of Jerusalem. He has come with a great army! As your father and I arrived to speak with King Hezekiah, his heart was considering removing the very gold from the doorway of the Temple itself. This he would have done to make payment to Sennacherib, that he might depart from our city and not bring harm upon us." Isaiah stopped talking just long enough to reach down and take another sip of the cool refreshing water in the cup.

Then he continued, "But this is not what the Lord instructed me to bring to the ears of our king, but rather, that no payment should be made! For God Himself will bring swift recompense upon Sennacherib's own head. For the Lord "spoke unto me saying; `there shall not be so much as one arrow cast from Sennacherib toward Jerusalem. But by the same way as he came, he shall also depart. For God shall come against him, and fight against him.`* These words I did share with King Hezekiah, and it brought his heart peace!"

The old prophet looked tired and well spent from his audience with the king, and having exhausted his spirit and mind with such a heavy address. Although Mishi heard everything the prophet had spoken, still his own heart needed convincing that they were safe. So he asked, "Were you able to see anything of the wicked king, and his army, has Sennacherib surrounded our city?"

"Yes my little friend," the old prophet responded. "His army now abides on every hill surrounding Jerusalem. But do not fear, for God will have his way with him." Mishi tried to picture the scene outside and how fearful all the residence of Jerusalem must be. In his mind he could see the torches of Sennacherib's army burning brightly all around the hills.

Jezreel sat down beside Mishi, and put his arm around his shoulder trying to comfort him. "Son when I was bid by the prophet to go up and speak with the King, my heart trembled within me. I was also afraid concerning this wicked king. But when I heard the prophet speak, he set my heart at ease. Mishi, God will take care of us! He has protected us and been our watchful keeper, he will not fail us." Mishi shook his head in thoughtful agreement and yielded himself to trust God once more.

It was early in the evening when the priest who was commissioned to keep them informed of happenings outside, entered the room again. Everyone stopped what they were doing to listen to his announcement. "Brethren, night has fallen, and the torches of the enemy draw nearer to the walls of our city. The armies of Israel are set in position to take arms, if Sennacherib should attack. But we will not trust in man, but rather in God who shall deliver us!"

After the priest left it wasn't long before movement within their fortress began to slow, as the weariness of worry and fatigue walked about taking them captive one by one. Many sat looking out into the room expressionless, lost in deep thought. Perhaps some were concerned about family or friends. Others had become numb to any sense of feeling.

A sudden stirring to Mishi's right caught his attention. He turned to see the prophet Isaiah, gently laying himself down on a bed mat, he too now surrendering to the calls of sleep. Mishi got up and walked over to him. As he stood above him, the prophet had the look of both man and child lying there wrapped together in one body. Isaiah's many years of age and gray hair portrayed his great wisdom. But the frailness of his body caused Mishi to feel the need of caring for him tenderly. He knelt down beside him, and slowly pulled some covering up over the weary messenger. The old prophet never moved or opened his eyes, he just laid there breathing shallow breaths, allowing his body to find rest.

When at last everyone else in the whole room was asleep but Mishi, he sat quietly listening to the sounds of breathing. He softly whispered to himself, "If I had to stay here long in this place I think I should go mad." He too lay down after many hours, trying to imagine what must surely be happening outside. Once again his imagination began to run wild. In his mind he could see Sennacherib, tall as the cedars of Lebanon stepping over the walls of their city. Then, he could envision the Lord of Host coming upon him as the prophet had said, taking him by surprise, and capturing him.

A faint smile came over his face, as the scene played out in his mind. With the evil king now a prisoner by his own thinking, he felt safe to close his eyes and find sleep.

It did not take long until he joined all the others in the room in restless slumber.

After a few hours his sleep became fitful, with his body wrestling to stay on the bed mat. Finally the covers under him became victorious in the struggle. He lay with his upper body on the cold flooring stones with his face against the pavement, but his lower body was not yet willing to concede defeat.

Then the stones began to beat and rumble beneath him, causing his teeth to shake in his mouth. His jaw bone took blow after blow from its pounding. He awoke to the sound of thunder rolling, like mighty rocks being tossed together. Like a giant whose feet was shaking heaven and earth as he walked.

"Abba, Momma," Mishi cried out in terror! They both quickly swept him into their arms and pulled him tight. He looked around the room at others who were holding on to one another for comfort. A clay vessel walked off the edge of the table and crashed to the floor, breaking into a million pieces.

"What is happening?" He cried! "Is it the wicked king? Has he come to take us captive?" Mishi clung to his parents so tight that his fingers ached with pain. People were screaming in the room, as they covered their heads from the rocks being loosened from above.

Then a voice began to speak above all the commotion in the room and just the sound of this voice brought calmness to them all. It was the prophet Isaiah! His eyes were turned heavenward as he spoke. "Hearken unto to me and hear what I have to say! It is not the forces of King Sennacherib which is shaking the earth tonight, but surely it is the Angel of God who walks over Jerusalem."

Within a few moments everything stopped. Nothing moved! No one in the room, it seemed, even drew a breath. They were too overtaken with fear.

Then they heard yelling.

It was someone coming down the hallway leading to the chamber. Someone close to the door quickly arose, ready to secure the doorway! But before the door could be closed, a swell of priest entered the room. Mishi looked through the maze of white robes to see a priest in the center of the company; the man's eyes were wild with fear! He was talking fast, and muttering in bewildered fashion.

"It was the Angel of the Lord," he kept saying over and over! "I saw him, filled with radiance and splendor as he moved across the whole of Jerusalem! His countenance was like a lightning bolt that flashed from the east to the west. He walked throughout the camp of the Assyrians, and with each step he shook the whole earth!"

The rest of the night was spent with anticipation of the breaking of day. No one could sleep anymore. People sat and talked, speculating about what might be found at the morning light. Every now and then, they would hear a moan, or rapid talk pouring forth from the priest that had witnessed the Angel of God. The others around him would comfort him until once again he became quiet.

When morning broke, word came down to them that many within the camp of the Assyrians had perished, and that Sennacherib was withdrawing his massive army, departing the same way in which he had came. They also learned that The Angel of The Lord had slew 185,000 men from Sennacherib's company.

By late that afternoon, Zadok appeared and they were all glad to know that he was safe. "You may once again return to your chambers, for Sennacherib's threat has now ended," he said. Everyone was relieved and thankful to know they would soon be leaving their underground hideaway.

Anna set about quickly to clean up the room that had served them these two days. She would not leave until everything was in order. When all was accomplished, and they were about to leave, Mishi turned to find Isaiah among the few still in the chamber with them. Jezreel walked over with him as he spoke to the old prophet. "Thank you, for your wisdom and heart of understanding," he said to him. "You truly understood the mysteries of God in this matter."

The old prophet reached over and laid his hand on Jezreel's arm, "Just you keep on proclaiming everything that God shall put in your heart, concerning your father," he said. Jezreel was about to thank Isaiah for his encouraging words when he noticed Mishi wiggling his way in between him and the prophet.

"Would you like to come and stay with us in our home chambers up on the Temple platform?" Mishi asked, taking Isaiah by the hand. The old prophet carefully knelt down on one knee so he was looking right into Mishi's eyes. "Now my son that I would love to do, but I soon will be taking my leave, returning to my own home. For I also am a scribe and I am compelled of the Lord to write many things that God hath spoken to me. But I thank you with all my heart for your most generous invitation!"

Mishi leaned in and wrapped his arms around him, holding him as tightly as he could. "I will miss you," he said. Isaiah gently placed his feeble hand on the side of Mishi's face. "Son you will do many great things for the Lord your God, and I am very proud of you," the old prophet said.

Jezreel took Mishi by the hand and began to lead his family out of the room which had served as their refuge. Zadok was waiting for them in the hallway, and they ascended the stairs up to the great Temple platform. When they arrived at the last step the door was opened leading out into the warmth and brightness of the sun. Mishi's eyes watered from the glare off the white stones surrounding them. But they were all glad to be free again, and to take in the fresh air which flowed over this holy place!

Chapter 10

Years of Friendship – A Thousand Memories

"Two friends sharing life together is far better than going through trials alone. Because, together they are able to produce far more results; if one falls down, his friend can help him. But pity the man who stumbles and has no friend to help him up!"

Ecclesiastes 4:9-10

After two days, the stench of death lay heavy in the air over the city. The massive army of Israel worked with fevered pace to bury the dead Assyrians as quickly as possible. Things at the Temple were beginning to return to normal. All the objects that had been carried down below had been restored to their proper places. And once again the priest's attention turned toward hearing Jezreel's account concerning the scroll that had been found.

On the third morning following the siege, he returned into the chamber. It was a somber mood within the room as the men entered and found their places. They had all been through much, both in body and spirit, over the last few days. The toil showed on their faces and in the movement of their step. You could see the weariness spilling forth in each man's motion.

When the high priest arrived, he also showed the long hours spent in anxious waiting and of protection over the House of God. He came and sat down by Jezreel, and then gave encouragement and instruction to all the priests gathered in the room.

"My dear brethren, I know you all have been through much in the last days. First, I wish to bless you for your faithfulness in caring for the vessels and all things here at the House of The Lord. God himself shall reward thee. Now I bid you take strength, and set your heart to hear more of the account from Jezreel, son of Hosea. For there is no other calling higher than this; that we preserve and care for the very Word of God. Once again we are being summoned to know if it has been the Lord who spoke through Hosea's scribed words."

As Jezreel began his narrative once more, he thought of the encouraging words Isaiah had spoken to him. He was assured in his heart more than ever that his father's words would be judged as a holy script! After all they had gone through, it felt good to be sharing again, the record of his father's life and the love he had for Gomer!

Having been given permission once more to speak, he now addressed the assembled priests. "As my father and mother left the Temple having performed the covenant of circumcision, joy filled their hearts. Walking the streets back to their home seemed like the very air around them was filled with the glory of God." Jezreel began!

✱✱✱✱✱✱✱✱✱✱✱✱✱✱✱✱✱✱✱✱

Hosea watched as the branches of the trees swayed in the wind. *"Even the trees are rejoicing with us,"* he pondered. The baby was still restless in Hosea's arms from the discomfort of pain, so he was careful as to how he held him. He certainly did not wish to place any more stress upon his precious son. Gomer walked beside her husband softly singing as she went, her face glowing with happiness.

She moved ahead of Hosea and in playful fashion turned and walked facing him, her feet moving backwards as she talked. "I will bare you many children, as many as your heart desires. And we will live all our days in love, and prosperity." She said as she whirled about in a dance like fashion. "It's the least that I can do for my grand deliverer!"

Hosea watched her, thinking how beautiful she was. She whirled about and moved along, portraying she had not one care in this whole world. It was like she had suddenly found the childhood which had been ripped away from her own life, because of her own rebellion. And now that little child within was being set free to enjoy life around her. Hosea let her dance and did not say one word to discourage her jubilation.

But just as he held his newborn son with great care to not bring any more pain upon him, he also knew that Gomer's frailness required such protection. Words from slanderous lips could pierce her very soul, and cause her happiness to be shattered in a moment's time. So he determined to hold her safe in his heart. He would carefully wrap her in the blanket of his love.

When they returned home that evening, the air had grown cool. As they approached the walkway leading up to their home, the smell of lamb being roasted over fire caught their senses. "That smells delicious!" Gomer said. Both of them had forgotten to eat anything in the business of the day. Hosea too was stricken with hunger from the inviting aroma now filling the air around them. He sniffed the air. "That smell makes one's very stomach wrestle within him, now doesn't it?"

As they walked inside the courtyard they saw Hosea's friend from next door, standing by the fire with a beautiful lamb cooking over it. "Welcome home my dear neighbors," he said gleefully. "I just thought we might need to have a little celebration in honor of today's covenant of circumcision."

Hosea and Gomer moved by the warmth of the fire and watched as Hosea's friend put the final touches to the meal. "This is absolutely wonderful, thank you so much for your thoughtfulness and kindness," Hosea said. Gomer whole heartily agreed. "If this meal had not been set in our home, we had determined by its wonderful aroma that we would find whoever it belonged to and steal it away from them!" She said. The friend let out a laugh. "Well I shall be more careful when I am preparing my food, lest it go missing at the hands of my very neighbors!" He said teasingly.

When all was arranged, the three of them sat down together. As they took bread, laughter and song filled the tiny courtyard. The food filled their bodies and the fellowship warmed their spirits. They talked about the day, and the naming of the child, and just how exciting the visit to the Temple had been.

Hosea's friend thought it was a perfect name. So, to show forth his approval of such a gallant name, he stood up and took a staff in hand. Looking stern faced he said, "All hail Jezreel!" You would have thought he was announcing the entrance of a king into his palace. All three of them joined hands and danced around the table, singing a melody of triumph. When the song was done, they almost fell to the ground with laughter.

"Shhhhh, be quiet you two crazy men," Gomer whispered. But it was too late; all the commotion had awakened the baby Jezreel, and he let out a cry. "I will get him, you all just stay right here and keep acting like two old fools," Gomer said. She got up and went inside to tend to the baby. The two men looked at each other once more, and started laughing until tears came down their faces.

Neither of them knew why they were laughing, it was just simply the joy from inside that made them crazy! Finally they regained their senses, and both went about cleaning up the mess. When it came time to leave for the night, the friend stopped and asked if he might look upon the child one last time. "Why, of course you may, just be quiet he is fast asleep," Gomer warned.

Hosea watched as his friend went into the house. He thought it strange that he would do this. It wasn't long until he returned, and bid them goodnight. As he got to the courtyard gate he said, "Hosea may I have a word with you please?" Hosea arose and joined his friend as they walked toward his home. "Certainly my dear friend, what is on your heart?" Hosea responded.

All the joyous expressions had now gone from his friend's countenance. He slipped his arm around Hosea's shoulder as they walked.

"In the morning I will be leaving our community, and I am not sure when or if I will be permitted to return." Hosea was perplexed by his friend's announcement. He stopped walking and just stood there hardly knowing what to say. He shook his head in disbelief. "But why, where are you going, and what do you mean, that you may not be permitted to return?" Hosea asked.

His friend looked away from Hosea. "I am so sorry, but these things I cannot make known unto you. All I can say is that I will be safe, and you have no worries concerning me." But Hosea was not yet willing to concede defeat in his questioning. "I know I will see you again, I must, for you have been a wonderful friend to me! What about your home, who will care for it?"

His friend began to unlock the door to his house while trying to answer Hosea's inquiry. "My home will be left here for me, if I return! But will you, my righteous friend, keep a watchful eye over it for me?" Hosea answered very matter of fact, "of course I will watch over your home! But who will watch over me, should I come home late into the night? And who will heckle me, and save me from the temptations of the darkness?" Hosea asked as the two men stood in the doorway.

He finally conceded that his friend had given him all the information he possibly could. And although his heart was breaking at the loss of such a lifelong companion, he still trusted him completely. Whatever the situation was that demanded his friend leave so secretively must be of great honor, Hosea concluded.

The two men embraced tightly, allowing years of friendship to flow between them. A thousand memories passed through their minds. They had been through so many things together! "I will never forget you," Hosea said, as he prepared to leave. Hosea solemnly walked the path away from his friend's house. Above the sounds of the night a gentle prayer drifted his way. He recognized the prayer and the soothing voice to be that of his dear friend.

"May the Lord bless you and keep you.
May the Lord make his face to shine upon you,
and be gracious to you.
May the Lord lift up his countenance upon you,
and give you peace."

Hosea did not look back, his heart would not allow him to, for the grief it would cause. But he knew the words his friend has just spoken over him; it was the words of the priestly blessing. Hosea had heard them many times as they were offered by the priesthood at the

Temple. He shook his head in saddened confusion as he walked the last few steps to his home.

　　As he arrived at the doorway to his own home, his heart felt empty. It had been a long day, starting with a celebration, and ending with separation. Gomer was already fast asleep, lying by the baby, tired from the day's activities. Hosea did not want to disturb her so he went upon the roof, and sat looking out into the night sky. The stars seemed to reach down and wrap their arms around him, to comfort him.

　　He stood there on the roof considering the final parting of his friend. *"The priestly blessing. Why would my friend speak the priestly blessing over me?"* He cast his eyes toward the home of his friend, and watched as the faint light in the window faded. Eventually it went out, and darkness invaded the one last presence of a friend who lived next door.

Chapter 11

Like A Dart Laced With Poison, Evil Words Find Their Mark

"Beware of fake prophets, who appear outwardly as righteous and caring people, but inside they are dangerous wolves."

Matthew 7:15

Gomer sat Jezreel on her hip, and lifted the bundle of clothes to the other side. "We will return in a while," she called out to Hosea, "after I am finished washing these clothes at the water pool." Hosea looked up from the table where he was sitting, writing on a parchment scroll. "I may be gone to preach by the Yarmulke River when you return." Gomer did not question this, for in fact she was glad; glad to see that her husband was feeling once again the call of God to preach. Off they went, in separate directions for the day.

The trip to the water pool was somewhat difficult for her. Carrying the baby on her hip and all the families' laundry in the other hand was never an easy chore. There were many women already gathered at the pool when she arrived. The heat from the late morning sun beat down upon her as its reflection glared off the sparkling water. She bent over to place the fabric into the cleansing stream. The water felt cool to her hands as each piece of cloth was aggressively agitated, removing the sand and grit that so easily imbedded itself into the fibers of the garments. Before starting her chore she had placed the baby Jezreel in his blanket and laid him carefully upon some of the clothing she had brought with her.

As she labored, a small voice spoke from behind her. She turned to see a little girl standing there, talking to the baby Jezreel. "Hi there", the little girl said. "My name is Gabriella, how would you like for me to be your friend?" The little girl sat down beside him innocently. Gomer left her washing and walked over to them and knelt beside the sweet visitor. "His name is Jezreel," Gomer said to her. The little girl looked up at Gomer and gave a brief smile and returned her attention to the baby. Gomer repeated the little girl's name out loud as she continued to speak to her; "Gabriella, that is a beautiful name and you are a lovely young lady." Gabriella's face lit up with bright radiance because of Gomer's attention paid to her. Gabriella reached over and touched Gomers long flowing black hair and returned a complement. "Your hair is so pretty, I hope when I grow up I can be as beautiful as you are."

Gomer felt a tinge of embarrassment run through her at the pure honesty of the child. Over the years many people had told Gomer how beautiful they thought she was. And of course hundreds of men had paid her compliments. But to have an innocent child give such a courtesy was unexpected and awkward for her.

She didn't have long to bask in the child's attention however, for Gabriella quickly turned back toward the baby once again. "May I hold him for a few minutes?" Gomer watched as Gabriella placed her tiny finger into the baby's innocent hand. He gripped it tightly causing Gabriella to erupt into giggling and laughter. "Sure you may hold him." Gomer encouraged, "we just have to be careful, for he is only a couple of months old."

Gomer tenderly slipped her hands under him and laid him into the arms of Gabriella. The young girl sat there gleefully, with her green eyes sparkling in the light of the sun. Her face glowed with a smile of complete satisfaction. "One day, when I am older I am going to have fifty children, maybe even a hundred!" Gomer couldn't resist a chuckle at the unrealistic wish of this angelic child. She casually repositioned the baby's blanket which had fallen loose due to his unrelenting squirms while Gabriella held him. Then she offered a loving word of encouragement to the dreamy eyed child. "My dear, no matter how many children you may have, I know you will be a wonderful mother someday."

A shadow appeared over them, and Gomer looked up to see Gabriella's mother standing above them. "There you are young lady," the woman said angrily. "Now you get yourself right back over there, to your chore of washing clothes, and stop wandering off like that!"

Gomer watched as the child's mother seized her hand and whisk her away. When Gabriella and her mother arrived back to the company of women gathered at the upper end of the water pool, Gomer witnessed the group erupt in whispered conversation. She was convinced from the sarcastic eyes being cast in her direction, that at least one in the assembly of women knew who she was and also knew of her past. Quickly the group of women began to scatter, moving as far away from Gomer as possible. They were pointing at her, and their faces showed bitter disgust. They moved away like a herd of gazelle, frightened by *the* lioness that had suddenly appeared at their watering hole.

Gomer began to clumsily gather her belongings and hastily she left. Feeling the resentment of these women hot against her neck as she walked, her mind went wild with anger and humiliation. Perhaps it was just her imagination that caused her to interpret their conversation as, "*Being against her.*"

Real or not, it brought a new realization into her spirit. In years past during her life of whoredoms, she had cared little about what others thought of her. But since meeting Hosea she had acquired some self-worth and now, it did matter how others perceived her. She had tried to mend her ways and walk a more wholesome path. As the distance between her and the women grew, so did the thoughts which multiplied in her mind. "*No matter how hard I try, I will never escape my past,*" she thought out loud.

Her steps carried her deep into the city before she even realized it. Her arms where aching from carrying the baby and the bundle of clothing. This throbbing in her arms is what brought her mind back to the present, away from thoughts of self-pity. In her distressed state of mind she hadn't noticed that all along the way she had been dropping some of the clothing from her bundle.

"Woman," an elderly lady called out to her. "You have lost some of your clothing!" Gomer stopped and turned around to see much of her clean laundry scattered over the dust covered pavement. She went over and stooped down to retrieve the misplaced garments. While doing so other items of fabric dropped to the ground. Gomer sat the baby down while she attempted scooped up her now stained laundry. All the while she was becoming more angry, and frustrated, and before she could stop herself, she swore violently. The words just came out! Her swearing and annoyance burst forth like waters from a damn that had been held tight for many days. Gomer was still in her crouched position while people walked around her as she went about attempting to regain all her goods. The dust from their sandaled feet tossed even more dirt on her clean garments.

As she arose from gathering both the baby and her clothing, she felt someone forcefully grab her by the arm. She turned her head quickly and stared into the face of Balak, one of her former lovers. "Well that sounds more like the Gomer I always knew, and certainly not the one I've been hearing of lately," he said in disgusting laughter.

Gomer looked down at Balaks' arm as it held tight to her own. It was bulging with muscle and strength. She had always thought him to be the very image of majestic itself: tall with a herculean body and a face so smooth it glistened.   His lips were full and could weave a tapestry of words, enough to entice the heart of any woman.

As Gomer stood there confounded by his unexpected appearance, scenes played out in her mind. It only took seconds for all their secret encounters to rush through her imagination. "Where did you come from?" she asked, "and please, turn loose of my arm!" Gomer demanded.

Balak released his grip and took a step back to look her over. "Where did I come from?" He said with a sneer and a laugh that sent shivers running up her spine. "I'll tell you where I came from! I have been out roaming to and fro, pacing here and there, looking for a woman as beautiful as you; one that could please me. I have searched, it seems throughout the whole earth, but there is none to be found as ravishing as you. I was seeking you, that I might devour you with my love and passion." Balak winked at her with an evil enticement.

Gomer could not move! It was as though her very feet had become embedded into the earth. She wished that Balak would stop talking, but he did not. Instead he continued to banter her with words that made her head spin. "Look at yourself! A woman that used to be carefree, making your own decisions. You have never had anyone to answer to, and no one for which you felt responsible. And now, you have the weight of a child sitting on your hip, and the load of dirty laundry trailing behind you as you walk."

Jezreel squirmed on her side, and let out a cry. She repositioned the baby on her hip. "Now you listen to me; for the first time in my life I do not have to worry about where I will lay my head each night. And, I have a man, a man that truly loves me for who I am, not for what I can give him. And now, I am going home to him, so I bid you farewell." Gomer whirled about and started to walk away. When Balak saw that his enticements did not snare her, he decided to plant a seed of doubt about Hosea and to share some news he had recently learned about her mother. So he struck out, like a bear with its claws sharp and deadly.

Balak called out to her. "And has it come to your ears the things your husband has spoken concerning you, in his sermons by the Yarmulke River?" Then without one ounce of mercy in his voice Balak continued speaking. "And I suppose you have no interest in knowing that your mother is sick and nigh unto death." At this Gomer stopped, and turned slowly back around, with her eyes burning as though they were on fire. "What things?" She asked. "What things did my husband say about me? And what do you know of my mother being ill?"

Balak smiled; the prey had returned to the bait! "Oh a few days ago I was passing by your husband's place of preaching and decided to stop and listen. I knew for him to be able to win your heart, he must be quite the talker. As he preached and prodded the people about their sins he happened upon the subject of adultery!" Balak stopped to make sure he had Gomer's full attention before continuing. "As he ridiculed them for their sinful ways someone from the crowd questioned him about his marriage to you, and why he a prophet of God, would take you - a whore, to be his wife!" Gomer walked closer now, very interested in what Hosea's response had been to this question. "And what answer did Hosea give to them?" She asked with a very inquisitive look. Balak tried to make his answer sound as truthful as possible. "Your husband said the ONLY reason he took you to be his wife was to fulfill a holy calling from the Lord."

Gomer pondered the answer, but already it stung like the bite of a viper. Then she remembered Balak's comment about her mother. "And what do you know of my mother," she asked. Balak once again raced for words in his mind. "I can only say that your mother is near unto death and has been asking for you. I sent word to her that I would find you and that I would bring you to her." From the lips of Balak, lying words had been spoken. And like a dart laced with poison they found their mark.

"If I choose to go see my mother I will go on my own, I do not need your help!" Gomer shot back. But she wasn't finished speaking just yet. "As for my husband's words about why he took me to be his wife, I will see to it that he answers for himself in that matter!"

She did not wait for Balak to say anything else! He had already said plenty, enough to stir her mind to confusion. "*Am I nothing more than a calling of the Lord to Hosea?*" Gomer thought to herself, as she walked the long road home that day. With every step, the small seed of doubt planted in her mind by Balak began to grow. She began to doubt Hosea's love for her. The old feelings of worthlessness were unleashed in her spirit like a pack of ravenous wolves. Gomer descended into the emotions of rejection, both from the women earlier in the day and now by the words of her own husband. Finally she spoke out loud, "I was such a fool to think the Holy Prophet Hosea could ever love someone like me, a wretched miserable woman of the streets!" Balak's cunning attack had come at the very moment she was most vulnerable. And By the time she arrived home she was sobbing uncontrollably.

****

When Hosea returned late that evening, he found Gomer hastily gathering belongings. The house was in complete disarray, with the clothing from the morning laundry flung about the room. He stood in the doorway, perplexity showing on his face. Gomer was still unaware of his presence as she moved about in a fashion that revealed the deep trouble in her spirit.

After watching her for a moment he spoke. "Is there something wrong? Why is everything thrown about in such disorder?"

Gomer was still turned away from him and putting items in a bag as she began to rant. "From the day I married you I have worried that my past would cast a shadow over your righteousness." She turned and faced him, with her hands flinging about wildly as she vented. "I always feared others would think me too unholy to be the wife of such a righteous man! And from the start, I was afraid you could never love me, simply for who I am. From the moment I met you every breath you take has been seasoned with prayer, and every decision you ever made needed the approval of your God. And today I find out that I am but one more righteous deed on your list of things to fulfill!"

Hosea opened his mouth to speak, but Gomer did not give him the opportunity to utter a single word. Her frustration continued to pour out. "God forbid that I only serve you as some `calling` from the Lord. Is that all our marriage is to you Hosea, just another righteous act?"

Her loud and boisterous words had caused baby Jezreel to become upset and he began to cry. She temporarily withdrew her focused glare of anger off Hosea, and moved to pick up the child. Her white long garment hung loose about her frame. In her knelt position the garment flowed down in front of her pulling it tight against her back. Hosea could see her body begin to shake. Her shoulders rocked with the weight of sobbing.

He walked over to her and gently laid his hand on her shoulder. But when she felt his touch she leaned her body away, so as to remove any comfort offered by him. Gomer held the baby as she dropped completely to her knees. She was rocking him sternly, with Jezreel's face lying against her neck.

Hosea tried desperately to keep his composure; he knew there had to be some misunderstanding in Gomer's heart. He carefully crafted his words in as gentle and soothing a voice as possible. "Gomer, I am so sorry for whatever has caused you to feel this way, but I just don't understand." He paused to see if she might respond, but only silence prevailed. "What do you mean that my love for you is just a righteous act, or that our marriage is only a calling from the Lord? Did someone tell you this?"

Gomer lifted herself up, the baby still in her arms, turning about once again to face Hosea. "Today, I happened to meet an old friend, Balak by name, and as he talked with me, he told me of coming to hear you preach, over by the River Yarmulke. He spoke of the people asking you questions, questions as to why you took me to be your wife."

Gomer's voice softened with sorrow, and she cast her eyes to the ground avoiding looking at Hosea any longer, for it hurt too much. With every ounce of strength she had left she confessed. "Balak said you told the people the only reason you took me to be your wife was to fulfill a holy calling from the Lord."

Hosea moved slowly as he reached over with his hand and softly moved it up and down her arm trying to comfort her. "Gomer, from the first time I saw you, my heart was captivated by you! You are in every breath I breathe! It was God who spoke you into my heart, and the love I have for you is completely pure! What this friend has spoken to you is just not true. You are far more to me than just a righteous deed. And you are the only woman I have ever loved. You must believe me! You must know how much I care for you. I would give my life if it would cause you to believe me now."

Slowly Gomer lifted her head and looked back into his eyes. "But how do I know which one of you to believe?" Hosea carefully placed her hand over his own heart as he answered her. "You must always remember, my love, truth should never be judged by words alone, but by the heart from which they come."

Gomer allowed a faint smile to show on her face, for she knew the heart of Hosea was pure. She began to shake her head gently, as in disbelief that she could have allowed herself to be deceived so easily. "I am sorry; I should have known you would never say anything like that. You have always shown me a heart filled with love from the night I first met you." She leaned over and put her arm around him, still holding the baby on her hip. A tear lay wet on her cheek, and was now transferred to the face of Hosea. He gently raised his hand to remove its moisture. "Gomer, every tear you shed, is no longer just yours, but instead, they are our tears. For when you weep, I weep with you, and when you sing and rejoice, so do I. Never forget this, please, never forget this!"

They both went about cleaning up the scattered clothes, and items left in disarray, due to her rampage. When evening came they sat quietly together on the roof. Gomer leaned against him, covered with a blanket for warmth against the chill of the night air. Hosea's arms wrapped tight around her, but few words passed between them. The sounds of the darkness encircled them and brought a sense of ambiance to the night. It comforted them.

Hosea looked across to the roof of his old friend's home and wished he was still there. If his friend had been around, especially on this day, he could have asked advice of him how to make Gomer feel more secure in his love.

Without warning Gomer broke the silence. "I don't ever think I will please them," she said out loud. Her words caught Hosea off guard. "Please who?" Hosea asked. He suddenly realized that in Gomer's silence she had been pondering many things. She spoke again, "the people! I feel the glare of their hatred every time I meet someone. Today while at the water pool, I felt like an outcast, like a leper stained with the scales of sin." Hosea pulled her close, wishing with all his heart he could protect her from the cruel fires of judgment.

A soft breeze lifted over the edge of their roof, and gently tugged at Gomer's black hair. "The air has the smell of rain in it," Hosea said. He started to get up, in an attempt to put some things away, out of the openness to the elements as the sound of light thunder rumbled overhead. In a moment the sprinkles began to fall. "We should move inside out of the rain," Hosea said. He turned to retrieve the hand of Gomer, to lead her down into the safety of their small home. But when he looked upon her face she just sat there, covers pulled up tight under her chin, with a smile on her face that foretold a mischievous thought.

"Have you ever been washed by the rain?" She asked. Hosea gave out a soft laugh, attempting to keep up with the mind of this woman. A mind that just moments before had the weight of the world on it, and now was racing fast down a whole new road of thought. "No," he answered with hesitation. "I cannot say that I have ever been washed by the rain. What in the world are you talking about?"

Gomer got up as though she was about to show him a whole new world, one perhaps he had never explored. She went about moving all the items on the roof to the edges of the walled surroundings, giving much space in the center. Hosea stood there watching her, as she laid the covers out flat on the roof. When all was ready she took him by the hand and bid him lay down by her. Soon they were lying on their backs looking straight up into the night sky. Hosea felt her hand slip into his.

"I used to do this," she said, "after a night of sinful encounters, if it was raining. I used to go out and lay down, letting the rain fall on my face." Hosea lay there looking compassionately toward Gomer. Then the rain began to fall more heavily as though it had all been written into the script. As it did, she whispered to him so no one else would learn this secret of getting their sins washed away.

As Gomer spoke she kept her eyes tightly closed. "I used to imagine that the rain drops - each one, was the very fingers of God gently running over my face, washing away all the guilt I felt within." Hosea let her talk, not wanting to interrupt the world in which her mind had entered.

"But tonight," she continued to whisper, "I am imagining the fingers of God are running over both our faces, washing away all the anger of this day! I can see them cleansing all the hurt between us, revealing only the love and hope that lies underneath." She squeezed his hand tight, her eyes still firmly closed. "Can you feel them Hosea, can you feel His fingers?"

Hosea softly whispered back. "Yes I can feel them! But I am not surprised the mighty hand of God is here at this moment." Gomer opened her eyes slightly, cutting them toward him in a curious fashion. "What do you mean, you are not surprised the hand of God is here?" she asked. Hosea reached over allowing his own fingers to trace the outline of her face gently. "God's hands are here because the most beautiful woman in the world is here. And that woman was fearfully and wonderfully made by His mighty hands. I suppose that He just had to come here tonight to visit her, and let her know just how very special she is to Him."

Chapter 12

She Has Gone to Sleep, in Eternal Peace and Rest

"Precious in Gods sight, is the death of a righteous saint."

Psalm 116:15

The next morning Hosea wandered outside; the rain had passed leaving the air damp and cool. He expected to find Gomer in the courtyard, for when he awoke she was not laying beside him. But, there was no fire burning for the morning meal, and Gomer and the baby were not to be found.

He quickly returned inside and looked to see if her belongings were in their place; nothing was amiss. *"Where could she be?"* He thought, concern rising in his heart. He went back outside and through the courtyard gate, calling out to her. "Gomer, are you here?"

As the search continued, he drew close to the home of his old friend. Softly he heard Gomer's voice call back to him. "We are over here; Jezreel and I are over here." Her voice had come from inside the home of Hosea's friend. He walked over and carefully pushed open the door and found her sitting inside. She was sitting on the dirt floor with her back to the wall, and her legs arched in front of her. The baby lay beside her on a blanket. Hosea stood there completely confused at finding her there. "What are you doing over here inside the home of our friend?" He asked.

"To think!" Gomer shot back, in assured tones. "I awoke early and the baby was restless. I did not want to disturb you, so I went walking and somehow ended up here." Hosea was concerned that her "thinking" might have taken her back to yesterday, and the things spoken to her from Balak. Whatever it was, her expression showed a determined confidence about it. A confidence that revealed the coming to terms with something deep inside ones very self.

Hosea wasn't sure that he wanted to know what her countenance revealed, but he sat down beside her none the less. "Tell me what is on your mind, what is it that is troubling you so early in the morning, to bring you this place of solitude?"

Gomer never flinched; she looked straight at him. "I wish to go and visit with my mother!" Hosea let out a sigh of relief. "Well, I am sure we can arrange for that," he said. "We will go as soon as you are ready!" Gomer got up and walked to the other side of the room as she spoke. "But I don't think you understand; I have not seen my mother in many years, and when I rebelled against her and left home for a life on the streets, she forbade me to ever return. But now, now that I have changed, perhaps she will see me again." Gomer's face glowed with hope and anticipation, that after all these years she might be reunited with her mother again. Yet, she dare not tell Hosea that it had been Balak who had stirred her heart to visit her mother.

Hosea arose and gathered the baby into his arms. "So, when do we leave?" At this, Gomer changed her countenance and the tone of her voice immediately. She purposely walked over and took the baby from his arms while speaking to him sternly. "No Hosea, this is something that I must do on my own! I don't think you realize the enmity I have caused between me and my mother. For once in my life I will make penance on my own. If you went with me, you would be pleading my cause. I can do this without you!"

Even though her words portrayed a good intention and purpose, they also seemed laced with brass insolence. Hosea had spent every waking hour caring for her, and providing for her every need. Now, her words of stern detachment made his heart ache. She did not give him long to ponder the estrangement before solidifying her intentions even more.

"In the morning, we will depart, Jezreel and I will go. For how many days I cannot tell, but it is something that I must do." Hosea knew there was no use to argue the point with her. Her mind was made up and as uneasy as he felt about her leaving, he also knew he must accept it.

Hosea went about the remainder of the day with many thoughts spinning through his head. He wondered what had brought on the sudden need of *"seeing her mother."* Perhaps her womanly instincts had somehow awakened the need of making amends. Or, greater still, he hoped it was all a part of maturity in Gomer and a desire to please

God. He shook his head in surrender. "Silly prophet, if you were to figure out the mind of this woman, then I should think Solomon in all his wisdom would pay thee honor!" He was in complete exhaustion from reasoning.

On the morrow when they arose, Gomer moved about in haste. Hosea's apprehensions had not lessened as he watched her gather the last few items with anxious enthusiasm. As he watched her prepare to leave, he somehow sensed that in her mind she had already made the journey. He felt that while in body she was still with him; in spirit she was already climbing the slopes of Mount Olivet.

"All is made ready," she said, walking into the courtyard. Hosea stood making his plea once more. "Why don't you let me come with you? It would be my pleasure to meet your mother, and to know that you arrive safe." Gomer's answer only served to deepen the misgivings within his heart. "Oh no, you can't," she said, hurriedly reaching down to pick up the last remaining items for the trip. "As I told you before, I am not sure what to expect from my mother, and I want to do this on my own." Hosea bargained with her; "well, at least let me walk you to the gate at the edge of the city." Gomer glared at him, agitated by his persistence. "Fine, if you feel you must, now come we must be going."

He chose to walk behind her, reluctant to show approval of her journey. Baby Jezreel smiled at him from over her shoulder as she walked ahead of him. When they came to the gate of the city looking east, Gomer stopped, and received all the bags from Hosea's hands. She lifted

Jezreel higher on her hip, and softly kissed Hosea on the cheek. "Now, don't worry, nor fret yourself, I will be fine, and I will see you in a few days." And with that she turned and started walking away, down the path leading across the Kidron Valley to the base of the Mount of Olives. The moment of parting had been cold, and with little emotion on her part. Hosea watched her and the baby as she walked the winding pathway leading up the base of Mount Olivet until a cluster of trees covered their view and soon they were gone, completely hidden from sight.

An emptiness lay in Hosea's stomach as he walked back home that day, attempting to reason out all the emotions he felt inside. But there were no answers which came, not even one. There was only one thing clear in his heart; it was love for Gomer, a love so strong Hosea believed they could weather any storm which might surface on the horizon.

Gomer's mother, Diblaim, lived on the other side of Mount Olivet, near the road leading to Jericho. The small village where Diblaim abode laid twice a Sabbath Days journey from the city of Jerusalem. As Gomer ascended the mountain, with baby and belongings in arm, she became winded from time to time by the laborious journey. The weariness brought on from carrying her load required that she stop often and rest along the way. The donkey path weaving precariously up the side of Mount Olivet gave her a lofty view of the city of Jerusalem from behind her. Occasionally she would turn around and just stand there looking out over its splendor. With each step, she moved further and further away from her home. It was noon when she finally reached the summit.

She found a large flat rock and sat upon it. Unlatching the leather strap wrapped around her ankles, Gomer carefully removed her worn sandals to allow her feet and legs to rest. Her stomach gnawed at her insides so strong it made her head spin. After several minutes of rummaging through her nap sack she located the victuals and a flask of water. The cool refreshing liquid was desperately needed on her dry and parched lips, and the food brought strength to her weary frame. As she sat, the heat from the midday sun beat down on her. She took a cloth and wiped the beads of moisture from her brow.

The baby had become fretful and began to cry so Gomer thought this was a good time to allow him to nurse. As she did, the intimate bond between mother and child caused her to speak to him tenderly. "Jezreel, your mother must find her way. I love your father, but I am not sure that I deserve him." She took her hand and caressed the baby's head as he took milk. "You see, your mother has not always been such a good woman. I have lived a wicked and evil life. I have been used by hundreds of men for their own pleasure. Until I met your father, it was the only life I knew."

Gomer continued to talk, as though the baby understood her words, as she allowed him to serve as her counselor. "It is the life that I loved to hate. The attention of men, the gifts they brought and the wild excitement of everyday survival." Suddenly she stopped talking and laughed at herself. "Like you can understand what I am talking about, little one."

It came time for her to depart and she took one last look at Jerusalem which lay behind her. In that distant view was the home she had come to know, her new life, and of course Hosea. And just ahead of her, down the eastern slope of Mount Olivet, lay the gateway to her old life. The winding path ahead of her would lead to the home of her mother from which she had been dispelled as a young girl, having chosen a life of whoredom.

Both paths called to her as she stood midway on her journey. Both roads spoke her name and both where visible from this lofty position. Her mind raced back to sitting in the home of Hosea's friend. It was there she had weighed the heaviness that comes with holy expectations. The fear of failure! These were the many thoughts that brought her to this crossroad and the wrestling with how to proceed.

When she had finished considering both, all that lay behind her, and the road set before her, Gomer turned and gathered all her belongings once more. "This will be best for Hosea," she said out loud. "The people are right, I am nothing but a harlot, and Hosea deserves better than me." And with that, she began to descend the mountain down to the other side.

It was late afternoon when she finally arrived at the tiny cluster of homes where her mother lived. The air was breezy, and carried the sweet smell of fruit from the orchards which dotted the hillside. As she wound her way over the dirt paths leading in between the homes, she began to feel like a child again.

Gomer had always been a spirited child, never one to just sit and play quietly. Most days she could have been found running as fast as she could through these streets with the other children from the village. It was funny she thought, "*I was always faster than everyone else, even the boys.*" A faint smile came over her face as she reflected on the distant memories. Then Gomer slipped off her sandals to feel the cool dirt road against her feet. "Ah, that feels nice," she said, as she started walking again.

As she walked, she met an occasional passerby; none of which, hardly acknowledged her presence. Just one elderly man she met stopped and came over to her. "That's a pretty baby you got there," the old man said, while reaching over and patting the child's head. "Thank you, his name is Jezreel, he is two months old." Gomer responded. The old man smiled widely, revealing a tooth missing on one side. None the less his countenance still glowed with joy and friendliness. But he did not linger; after he had spoke to her with gentle praise, he moved on down the path.

In behind some homes to Gomer's left, rose many fig trees, each row terraced, one, a little higher than the other up the side of the hill. Their huge twisted limbs swayed in the stiff breeze. "Almost there," she said out loud, her heart starting to pound inside her chest, nervous with anticipation.

"*Seeing ones mother for the first time in many years is not an easy task; just take a deep breath and calm yourself.*" She counseled her own spirit. The journey had been long, but with one last turn she was standing in front of her childhood home. Gomer sat her bags on the ground while nostalgically taking in the scene.

It was like a painting, etched on canvas. Her mother's home sat tight against the base of the mountain with a stone wall about waist high running up to it on either side. Flowers hung over the edge of the stones in grand clusters. The courtyard was hidden behind a carefully laid wall that stood a bit higher than her head. And from these blocks hung vines matted with flowers in colors of blues and yellows. Birds sung playful melodies in abundance all around, perhaps feeling safe and finding refuge in the tall trees covering the country side. As she stood there taking in the image, a dog rushed around the corner of another house nearby. He was in pursuit of a flock of chickens, which was squawking and flapping their wings wildly. All of them together flowed around Gomer and Jezreel like water around rocks. But it had been enough to awaken her mind back to the present.

Taking a deep breath, she placed her foot on the step leading up into the courtyard, and entered inside. "Shalom, is anyone here?" She called out, but no one answered. Gomer moved deeper inside, leaning around each corner slowly and carefully. "Shalom, mother, are you in here?"

When no one responded from the courtyard, Gomer walked to the door, laid her hand on it gently, and gave a faint knock. When no one responded, she tried the latch, and found it to be locked. "Hmm," she said, "must be in the orchard, come on little fellow, we will find her."

Gomer moved in behind the house and entered the terraced vineyard, and found baskets sitting on the ground, showing evidence of someone present. She climbed a little higher as the sound of singing began to fill her ears. At the end of one of the rows she stooped down to look under the canopy of fig trees. Gomer could see a woman standing with her back to them, but the woman was shorter in stature than Gomer's mother. The fleshly-looking woman was singing a lonely melody while her arms moved in precise rhythm, picking figs from the limbs above her head.

Gomer could see that the woman's hands were wrinkled and her fingers drawn with age. Her head was covered, in a godly fashion, but the garments she wore were brightly colored, and matched the atmosphere of the vibrant countryside perfectly. A stiff wind came down the slope and picked up the basket the woman was using, sending it rolling over to where Gomer was standing. It now lay at her feet! The woman turned quickly in an attempt to catch it, but it was too late, the basket had escaped.

"Oh my, you gave me a fright young lady," the woman said as she walked over to retrieve her missing hand woven assistant. "The figs won't be ready for a while yet, is there something else..." then she stopped mid-sentence, as she looked Gomer over in curious fashion. As her eyes began to widen, her wrinkled hand was brought to her lips and covered her mouth in surprise. "Oh Lord of my father's," the woman spoke in surprise. "Is it truly you, Gomer, which stands before me?"

Upon seeing the woman's face closer, Gomer recognized her to be Serah, a neighbor of her mother who had lived nearby for many years. "Yes, it is I," Gomer said, unsure of how to respond at Serah being in the vineyard instead of her mother.

"I have come to know the well-being of my mother, and to find my way with some things." Gomer spoke cautiously. Serah moved closer, and wiped her hands on an apron before embracing Gomer and the baby in one loving grasp. No sooner had the feeling of joy began to overtake Gomer at this reception, Serah stepped back, as though she dreaded the next words she must speak.

"Child, your mother has fallen ill, and abides at my house. I have been caring for her. She took sick about three months ago, well stricken with years and worry." Serah laid her hand on Gomer's face as she continued. "But it is good that you are here child, for she may not last another day."

Gomer searched Serah's eyes, "is momma able to speak, and will she know that I have come?" Serah shook her head softly; "no child, she has no strength for words, and even now the rattles of death are upon her."

Serah realized that Gomer might wonder why she was in the vineyard, while Dibliam lay near death, so she began to explain. "I only came to the vineyard with haste, in hope that we might convince her to take some of the sweetness of the harvest and gain a little strength." Serah's attention turned to the baby. "And who might I ask is this little one?" Jezreel smiled widely as the old lady's hand tenderly teased at him. "This is my son, Jezreel, he is two months old." Gomer said proudly. The baby laughed as Serah's hands pleasantly touched his cheeks.

As Serah and Jezreel enjoyed one another's company Gomer suddenly felt the need of defending her right to bear the child. Even though Serah had not interrogated her with a single question regarding the matter, Gomer willfully explained. "I am now married, to the most wonderful man you could ever imagine." But just as quickly as she shared this purposeful news she also cast her eyes downward. "But I am afraid my being married is the true reason for my coming here." Gomer expected Serah to question her about all these recent changes in her life, but instead she quickly pulled Gomer's mind back to the urgency of the hour.

"My, my, we better pick some of this fruit and get back to the house, so you may see your mother," Serah said. Both women set about putting as many figs into the basket as quickly as they could. Both knew how much these vineyards meant to Dibliam, and felt it only right to have such an important part of her life close by in these final hours.

When they arrived back at Serah's house, other women were already present, helping tend to Dibliam. As they saw Gomer enter, they all greeted her with the same amazement and warmth that Serah had offered. There were joyful words and greetings exchanged between them, and everyone wanted to hold baby Jezreel. He went from person to person, being passed with much fuss made over him.

Soon Serah took Gomer by the hand and gently led her into a room, set deep in the back of the house, where her mother lay. The room was dimly lit, with soft rays of light, reaching through the boarded window. Her mother lay flat on her back, with the covers pulled up to her neck, tight, as though little movement had taken place to disturb them. The figure of her mother's small frame was barely visible through the white linen that lay upon her body. Her hands were laid one on top of the other, and rested on her stomach on the outside of the covers. Gomer walked closer, and watched as Dibliam slowly took one shallow breath after another. She wanted to touch her mother's face, but instead she softly leaned down and kissed her hands. Dibliam's mouth was slightly opened, and her eyes had the look of death in them as she stared straightway toward the heavens. Her hair was long, and gray, and hung down over the front of her shoulders.

Gomer felt the hand of Serah gently take her by the arm. "If you wish child, after you take some bread, and nursed the baby, you may come and sit with her as long as your heart desires." Gomer gently laid her head on Serah's shoulder and felt tears coming to her eyes. "Yes, I would love to do that," she said, and both the women quietly slipped out the doorway.

As they took bread and conversed one with another, Gomer's mind often drifted back to her mother. She was glad she had came, even if other things were heavy upon her heart, she was still glad they had brought her here at this important time. Afterward she nursed Jezreel, and gently laid him down fast asleep on a bed mat Serah had provided. "Don't you worry about him child, we will all watch after him. Now, you get on in there and be with your mother," Serah told her.

Gomer was soon pushing back the curtain doorway and quietly entering the room where her mother lay. Gomer slipped off her sandals, to get comfortable, as she sat in the floor by the bed. She reached over and took her mother's hand in her own; bringing it closer to the edge of the bed, near where she sat. The hand was already cool to the touch, and felt stiff. Gomer ran her fingers over it, feeling the loose skin on the back of Dibliam's hand. Gently she slipped her fingers into her mother's, and brought the hand to the side of her face.

"Mother, it's me Gomer. I have come to see you, and I am very sorry you have taken sick. I stopped by the house and the vineyard. Oh how beautifully you have cared for everything! I saw the trees and the flowers hanging over the walls, and I even visited the orchard, and my how the trees have grown. Mother, I know many times I have disappointed you, and was very rebellious against you. It wasn't your fault, for you have always been a wonderful woman, as godly as any in all the land of Israel. If you only knew how many times I have wished to be like you! To live as good, and pure as you, but somehow I always failed to live up to your standards."

Gomer paused as though she had caught sight of something good inside herself, something that might make her mother glad if only she knew. Gomer looked up at her mother. "You would be proud of me," she continued. "For once, I can honestly say you would be proud of me. Mother, I am married now, and you have a grandson, and his name is Jezreel! And the man I married, well mother believe it or not, he is a prophet. He is a good man, a wonderful man in fact! He is good to me mother, far more than I ever deserve. Oh if only you could talk to me, and tell me what I should do! For you see, if I could be like you, and always do what is right, then yes I might be worthy enough of this man. I know I have done terribly wrong and hurt so many people. It is this deep-seeded wrong that causes me to wonder now, if I am good enough to be with this wonderful man. I call him, *My Grand Deliverer*! It is my own heart that struggles with this guilt. My husband has never done anything to cause me to feel this way. I just don't wish to cast a shadow on him! Why is it so hard for me to live righteous? Even now, my past calls out to me, the familiar, and the ways which are common to me."

Then Gomer broke into weeping. "I never remember in all my life telling you this, but, I love you, I do love you, and I am so sorry for hurting you! And now if only you could somehow speak to me, or let me know in some way that at least you hear me, and that you forgive me, then my heart could find some healing."

Gomer arose, half sitting and half kneeling, in an urgent attempt to be cleansed. "If you can hear me just please, grasp my hand tight; then I will know you have forgiven me."

Gomer held on to her mother's hand, until the weariness of the watch finally rocked her to sleep. She laid her head over onto the edge of the bed and gave in to the calls of fatigue. It was near morning, when something awoke Gomer, it was a tight, firm grip on her hand. Over and over her mother's fingers grasped the hand of Gomer. At the realization of her mother's decisive movement Gomer became overjoyed. "You heard me didn't you?" She beamed with excitement. "You knew I was here!"

Gomer rushed out to get Serah, and make known to her the response from her mother. But as the two women reentered the room, Dibliam lay completely silent, with no sound of breathing. Her eyes were fixed, with no sight in them. Serah placed the back of her hand softly in front of Dibliams mouth, but there was no breath. After what seemed like an eternity Serah softly looked over at Gomer. "She's gone child. She has gone to sleep with her fathers, in eternal peace and rest." The two women embraced, allowing comfort to flow between them.

Chapter 13

Nothing but Guile Ever Came From His Mouth

"We are not to be like immature children, persuaded by everything we hear, by the trickery of men, by craftiness and deceitful plots."

Ephesians 4:14

"...for there is not one word of truth in him (the Devil). When he speaks, he is lying, because he is the father of lies."

John 8:44

After the passing of Dibliam, Gomer stayed at the home of Serah for the next few days. They discussed many things, the past, and how it could have been different, the present, and how Gomer wished to find her way with it, and the future, for her and the vineyard which had belonged to her mother. "Someone will need to tend to it," Serah explained. "I am getting too old, and there is no one else of her heritage but you child."

Serah was sweeping the dirt floor with a straw broom as she continued to talk. The dust arose in the air, causing the room to darken with a slight haze. Gomer tried to contain a cough as long as she could, but finally the particles of dust overpowered her. She snatched up the baby and made a dash for the door. Outside she took a long cleansing breath as her coughing began to subside. Serah soon appeared. "My goodness child," she began to scold. "If you are going to be a homemaker you will need to be far more tenacious than that." Gomer coughed up the last remaining grains of grit as she defended herself. "Well, I didn't know being a homemaker included being strong enough to swallow a bucket load of dirt."

Both women laughed as Serah made a place for them to sit down. She propped the broom across her lap as her expression of laughter slowly changed. "Gomer, speaking of you being strong, there is something about the vineyard I think you should know. Many years ago, we experienced a harsh draught. Due to this, and for your mother to retain the rights of ownership of the vineyard, she incurred a large debt. Over the many seasons she was able to repay some of this liability. But in more recent years the harvest has been small, and then she became ill."

Serah leaned more heavily, placing her arms on the broom for support as she divulged more information. "If you should decide to remain at the vineyard, you should be aware, that there have already been collectors coming around asking for money against the property." This was the last thing that Gomer needed to be facing now, and she knew it. She had already been contemplating the possibility of staying at the vineyard for a while as a means to buy time away from Hosea, and to ponder the many things that weighed heavy on her mind.

On the sixth day after her mother's death Gomer went to stay at the home of Dibliam. *"Only till I can get things settled,"* she had told herself. After receiving the key from Serah, Gomer walked the short distance to her mother's home and slipped it into the lock. The door opened slowly on its leather hinges. The house looked so much smaller to her than she remembered when she was a child. As she stood in the doorway the sorrowful scene of the day when she had left so long ago played out in her mind. The terrible insults she had screamed at her mother as she walked out the door echoed in her ears. But now the house was almost silent, only a window covering gently flapping in the breeze could be heard.

To the right of the door as she entered was a wall with many shelves on it. Jars, and vessels, filled with spices, and grains occupied the narrow ledge. Gomer examined each one carefully, tasting some of the contents, to know if they were still good. "Oh my," she made a terrible face, "Garlic powder!" In disgust she turned to spit it out on floor, as she would have done in times past, but then remembered where she was. Her mother would scold her terribly for such a deed. *"Must be lady- like,"* she thought. So she quickly made a dash for the door and spat it out onto the ground. "There, that's better," she said feeling proud of herself and her behavior.

She found the clay fire oven sitting in a corner, and it looked as though it had not been used in a long while. Gomer summarized that since Dibliam had been at Serahs so long, no one had been here at all. She carefully picked up the oven and carried it outside for cooking on later. Upon reentering the house she noticed there were white bags sitting around the base of the walls. She untied the rope laced tops and found them to be filled with dried figs, and apples. In the center of the room a curdling sack hung from the ceiling, for making cheese.

After exploring for a while she found that most things within the house were unfamiliar to her. Only one thing in the whole room had not changed. It was a small wooden table with three seats tucked neatly underneath. On the table sat five clay oils lamps with the old flax wicks still hanging out the ends. A look came over Gomer's face, one that showed a distant memory. She got down on her knees to look up under the chairs. After searching under the first two, she finally found what she was looking for. There, underneath one of the chairs, was a burnt place, blackened by fire. As a child she crawled under here with an oil lamp, to test its flame on the chairs wooden bottom. Her curious behavior had almost caught the chair on fire. "Yes, I took the rod of correction for that one," she said out loud.

There was another room in the house set back through a doorway, much like that of Serah's, where her mother had lain. In this room Gomer found mats rolled up, and in one corner, leaning against the wall, were tools used in the orchard. A small divan provided a place for the bed mat to be laid upon. Gomer was very much ready to put it to good use by day's end. All the straightening and exploring of years gone by had left her tired and weary.

As she lay down her mind was set adrift. She wondered about Hosea, convinced he must surely be very concerned over her delay in returning home. It had been seven days since Gomer had left him standing at the gate of the city. She longed to feel his arms wrapped around her once again. She let Hosea's face come into her mind, as she looked at Jezreel lying close beside her. "You are the image of your father," she said with a growing forlornness.

Sounds of darkness began to fill her ears, and the cold loneliness of night crept in, overtaking her. It had been so long since she had slept in this house, and it had also been quite a long time since she had been so alone. Ever since the night when Hoesa had found her, near the broad wall with that stupid donkey, she had not been alone. A smile came over her face as she rehearsed the memory of that night in her mind.

"My grand deliverer!" She said out loud. Just hearing herself speak that little phrase went deeper into her soul, than she could have anticipated. It made her long for Hosea now more than ever. *It is quite amazing how much you miss someone when they are not around*, she realized, as she lay there. "We must return home little one. Your father must be worried sick about us. In the morning we will go home, and make him aware of all that has happened; of mother and the concerns of debt about the vineyard. He will know what to do!"

Gomer drifted into slumber with visions of walking the road back across the mountain and just how difficult it would be. She remembered the way her legs and body had ached from the weariness of the first journey across. But her dreams also transported her home, and there standing at the gate of their house was Hosea, peering out into the night. She could see his face, his brow all wrinkled with worry. She wanted to speak to him, to let him know that she was alright. But in her dream world her voice was silent!

The next morning dawned with a feeling of nervous anticipation in her spirit. She did not linger very long in preparation. It was just breaking dawn when Gomer finished gathering the items for the journey. By leaving so early she could forego much of the day's heat. "Come on little one, let's go home to papa." She said to baby Jezreel.

As Gomer opened the door and peered out into the morning haze, she could not believe her eyes. There, sitting in the courtyard, was Balak warming by the fire oven. Gomer shook her head to know if she was still dreaming or if the scene could be real. "What are you doing here? How is it that you sit by the fires of warmth in my mother's courtyard so early in the morning?"

Balak leaned forward lifting his palms toward the fire, calmly and unconcerned, as though this was the one place in the whole world he was supposed to be. He never even looked up in her direction as he spoke. "Gomer, I was sure you would come here to visit with your mother. Is it such a terrible thing that I would attempt to know that you had arrived safely?" Once again the same paralyzing sensation overtook her, like she felt the day she went to the water pool and encountered Balak. Gomer took a step backwards, keeping a safe distance; not because she feared he would try to cause her harm in body, rather that she feared what he might do to her spirit if she yielded herself too close.

"And just how did you come to learn that I was here, and how did you find your way to my mother's vineyard?" Gomer asked with cautious intent. Balak slowly turned his head to glance at her from over his shoulder. "Oh I have my ways; have you forgotten how cunning and crafty I can be? You always thought that was one of my better qualities."

Although Balak's words were laced with raw evil and deceit, it was the kind of words that Gomer was most familiar with. She had lived her life by them! Deceiving and being deceived! It was like a game; outsmart the hunter and you shall live.

Gomer knew she had to get away from the enticement of Balak's words. She knew that nothing but guile ever came from his mouth, and if she listened long enough they would confuse her mind. "Well you may stay here in the courtyard and warm yourself all you wish. But as for me and my baby, we were just leaving."

Gomer walked past Balak, knowing that this was what she should be doing. But inside, secretly inside, a war was being waged! She wished that Balak would call out to her and bid her wait. Maybe just ask her to stay a moment longer and talk with him. Oh, she knew it was wrong, but the overwhelming chore of making a right decision in the midst of temptation was never one of her

best qualities. Because of this, she walked passed Balak
and through the courtyard gate in bold defiant pretense.

Just as she stepped beyond the doorway her eyes
immediately caught sight of something to her left. It was a
large figure which flinched wildly, having been frightened
by her presence. Gomer stopped, to make sure her eyes
were not fooling her; for there, standing tied up near the
courtyard wall, was the most beautiful white horse she
had ever seen in all her life.

Gomer walked over carefully so as not to frighten
the animal any more. "Hi there," she said, gently running
her hand down his side. Unlike moments before when she
had frightened him, now he stood ever so still, only giving
a slight twitch of muscle on the side of his broad neck.
"What's your name big fellow?" Gomer asked, now
captivated by the massive beast standing before her.

"The stallion's name is Tryphon," Balak said,
having positioned himself in the doorway behind Gomer.
She quickly brought her hand to her chest, "you
frightened me!" she said. "Who does he belong to? Surely
he is not yours, for I have never known you to own such a
glorious beast of burden."

Balak walked closer to them now. "You know,'" he
said, "you are right, I don't deserve an animal so majestic,
and you're also right that he doesn't belong to me. Instead
he belongs to one as fair as the morning surrounding us.
He is yours Gomer, he now belongs to you. With one
condition being met and he is all yours."

The last time she had heard those words was when
she and Hosea had bargained over the donkey tied up in

his courtyard. But her mind quickly summarized there was no comparison to that stupid animal and this royal stallion. Once again in her heart she knew the right thing to do would be to run, just turn and run as fast as her legs would carry her, carry her away from Balak and the wonderful animal before her. The animal that she knew could ease the burdensome trip across the mountain. The animal that could make the journey so much more quickly than her own legs could take her.

Gomer conceded, "So, tell me, what condition shall make him mine?" Balak smiled at her with confidence, knowing the trap he had set was about to ensnare his prey. "All that I ask of you is this; that you would allow me to escort you back across the mountain to your husband. For you see Gomer, even though you belong to another, I still care for your well-being and your safety." He paused briefly as though he were gathering one final assault of words, with which he would entice her. "When we arrive in Jerusalem, if your heart bids me leave, then I will do so!"

Gomer stood looking at him, pondering his invitation. It seemed innocent enough. "*What harm could there be in that? Besides it will only serve to bring me to Hosea that much sooner.*" She gave a thoughtful nod of her head in acceptance of Balak's offer. "Because of the swiftness of the stallion, I shall I accept your offer! And, that he might take me to my husband with great speed and promptness." Gomer watched as Balak walked back around to her and locked his fingers together while positioning himself to assist her upon the powerful steed.

It felt awkward, yet strangely satisfying to Gomer
as she was led away with Balak at the helm. She adjusted
Jezreel so that he was partially lying against the horse's
neck, and relieving her of the strain of holding him. As
they moved into the tiny roadway leading back through
the cluster of homes, few people were stirring at this early
hour. However, as they neared the edge of the village,
more people became visible. As the rhythm of the horse's
steps gallantly strode along, she felt a sense of pride rise
up within her. Few people had she ever seen riding a
stallion so majestic, as the one Balak said now belonged to
her.

After a while of riding, Balak stopped the
procession right in front of a merchant shop filled with
breads, fruits, and sweet pastries. He walked over to
examine the many wonderful smelling treats lying before
him. "Give us some of those, and yes we will take plenty of
your sweet cakes," he said, pointing out to the owner
which of the treats he desired. "Nothing but the best for
the beautiful lady on the horse," he spoke again, as though
Gomer were a queen, and he, her royal servant.

The shop keeper lifted his eyes, to look at her, and
then set about to fill the order. When all was finished,
Balak walked back over and handed up to her much of the
sweet and tasty purchase. "There you are my fine lady,
food for the journey!" Gomer gave him a subtle smile and
thanked him. But the food only served to enhance the
feeling of grandeur, which by now was overtaking her.

As they made the journey out of the village and
started to ascend the Mount of Olives, Balak began to

talk. He talked on and on about the past, and the many times they had been together. He spoke of how much he had loved her, and how much joy and pleasure she had brought to him. He talked of the area of the broad wall, and of many old acquaintances; people Gomer had known over the years. He spoke of how she belonged among *"those people"*. His words kept coming, pouring forth in hypnotizing fashion as he talked on and on until Gomer became mesmerized by the enticing words.

When they broke the crest of the mountain with Jerusalem now lying in front of them, Balak stopped the horse. He came over to assist Gomer in dismounting from her lofty position. His strong arms reached for her as she gracefully slipped into them. Balak carefully delivered her and the baby safely to the ground. Gomer stood between the horse and Balaks masculine body. As they stood there, their eyes met in a long dreamy stare until Gomer finally found the strength to look away. Balak tenderly brushed her hair away from her face. "Let's rest here for a little while," he said. He led her over to the same rock where she had sat and nursed Jezreel, days before.

Balak tied up the stallion and walked over to sit beside Gomer. "You know, it would be so wonderful to feel you in my arms once more. Do you remember all the good times we have shared; times of love, and wondrous passion? We could have been so good together! Ours would have been the life of romantic adventure! Gomer, that is who you really are, a woman of free spirit and wild sensuality!"

Gomer looked to speak, perhaps in an attempt to save her own soul from the barrage of words that kept pounding deep into her head. But as long as she listened, the crafty words slowly and carefully chiseled away at the woman she had become, only to unveil the woman she used to be. She opened her mouth once again to speak, but no words came out. Finally in a voice made weak from the heaviness of temptation she whispered, "Balak," but that was all she could speak. Before she could say anything else, his hand found its way to her face. Softly and ever so tenderly the hand of Balak cupped the side of her face. Slowly his fingers moved carefully, tracing the outline of her lips. And without warning he leaned over and gently kissed her. His lips felt hot as they touched her own. Gomer closed her eyes allowing the sweet taste of the kiss to engulf her mind and body. Her hand slowly took hold of the back of Balak's arm. She could feel the muscle bulging tight down the back of his flesh. And in that very moment she felt her soul release the Gomer she used to be, wild and untamed.

Chapter 14

The Power of Grace and Love, the Innocent Seeking and Saving the Guilty

"The Messiah suffered for our sins, **the just for the unjust**, that He might reconcile us to God, because of His death in the flesh, we are made alive by the Spirit."

1 Peter 3:18

By the time Gomer and Balak arrived at the gates of the city of Jerusalem, a cunning plan had been devised. Gomer would take Jezreel home to Hosea under pretense of staying, and in a few days she would slip out deep into the night. Leaving the baby in the safety of Hosea's care would at lease ease her conscience somewhat. In her heart she knew what was right, having been raised under the godly influence of her mother. But in Gomer's mind a floodgate of temptation and seduction had been opened, and once allowed to breach the walls of righteousness, it became a raging torrent!

Once the plan was completed Balak gave her the final instructions. "I will be waiting for you at the Eastern Gate! Be sure to flee under the cloak of darkness so our deeds will not be found out," he told her.

They glanced around to make sure no one was looking in their direction as Balak leaned over and kissed her lips before departing. As his posture re-straightened, suddenly and without warning he was hit on the side of the face by what seemed to be a rotten melon. Both Gomer and Balak were completely overcome with surprise as once again they surveyed their surroundings in bewilderment. As Balak wiped the juice from his eyes, allowing his vision to focus, Ishtob the market keeper came into full view. How they had missed seeing him before the kiss, neither of them could figure out. Ishtob had launched the melon from a cart laden with over ripened fruits and vegetables. And now he was standing beside the cart with his feet firmly positioned so as to allow him the ability to cast another weapon of anger, should either of them attempt to move.

While keeping both of them firmly in his sight, Ishtob reached down and picked up another rotting weapon. His hand was drawn back ready to toss it at a moment's notice as he began to rant at them. "You both should be stoned to death!" He said. "I knew from the day that Hosea took you to be his wife that it was only a matter of time until you would break his heart. Gomer, do you even care that for the last few days your husband has been out looking for you from morning till dusk? He has been worried sick about you! I thought you had gone to your mothers, but instead I find you here with this sorry excuse for a man."

Balak raised his hand to speak, now angered and embarrassed that his masculinity had been challenged by the lowly market keeper. But Balak's arrogance only served to bring on an assault of rotten melons. Ishtob launched a massive attack! With lightening speed the market keeper flung one stinking missile after another, each one hitting their target perfectly.

Balak was seething with anger, but could do little. For every time he would attempt to move his feet, they slipped on the mess, casting him to the ground. He finally managed to position himself on all fours and scurry off. He looked like a weasel slipping and sliding away from some animal about to devour him.

Balak escaped his terrible ordeal, leaving Gomer to fend for herself. Gomer stood silently, looking at Ishtob expecting his assault to be turned on her next. In one arm she held baby Jezreel while in the other hand she held tight the reign of Tryphon the horse. But to her surprise, Ishtob slowly dropped the melon meant for her back into the cart. His eyes, which just moments before had burned with fury, now softened with sadness. He wiped his hands off on his garment and spoke to her, like a father speaking to his own daughter that had gone astray. "Gomer, how could you do this? You have the most wonderful husband in all the land of Israel. How could you deceive him like this? Instead of over ripe melons falling on your head, you know it could be stones raining down on you."

Ishtob paused as a sudden realization swept over him. He was in a dilemma. A terrible dilemma! If he allowed Gomer to return home and the people found out about her unfaithfulness, he was sure they would stone her to death. Their hatred for her was already at fevered pitch.

It was Gomer that broke the tension. "I cannot bear to look into the face of Hosea," she said with her head bowed in shame. She raised her head slightly as she took a few cautious steps toward the good market keeper. Her mouth was dry with nervousness. "Ishtob you must hear me, you must listen to me, for it is not completely as you have seen." By now she was standing right in front of Ishtob as she placed her hand on his chest, pleading her cause. "Yes, I know that I have done terrible wrong, however, you must believe me when I say I love Hosea with all my heart. I know that is hard for you to believe now, I just felt for his own sake it would be ...better if I..." Her words faded, knowing that it was all far too complicated to even try and explain.

Her eyes searched for mercy and understanding in Ishtob, perhaps there was some way he could feel her pain and regret. She raised her head to look at him once more, and resolved that there was only one thing she could do to show any love for Hosea, and even this decision she was about to make could be judged evil of her.

"Would you be so kind to take my son home to his father?" She said. "I will not allow him to lose both of us. Please Ishtob; see to it that Jezreel is safely delivered back to Hosea. And no matter what you believe, will you please also tell him this; that I do love him, and I am so sorry for hurting him."

By now Gomer was weeping uncontrollably as she laid Jezreel into the arms of the gentle market keeper. Once the baby was safely transferred, Gomer stepped back and looked upon her sweet little boy. She gently caressed his hair. "Goodbye little one, I promise I will see you again, I promise! I love you Jezreel and I am so sorry for hurting you also!"

She kissed the top of the baby's head as her tears poured down like an overflowing river. Ishtob never moved! He was frozen with responsibility. Gomer quickly turned away from them and ran away as fast as possible. Ishtob watched her until she was completely out of sight.

Immediately his mind went to the well-being of the baby he held in his arms. He knew he must get Jezreel home to Hosea, but that also meant facing the prophet with the news that would break his heart. Slowly he began to walk the road into the inner city, thinking all the while how strange it felt for him, of all people, to be carrying a baby. And, he was glad, very glad, that few people were mingling about to see him in this dutiful dilemma.

As he walked, Ishtob held Jezreel tight against his chest, his big hands covering the baby's eyes to keep the bright sunlight from hurting them. He had left the fruit cart, thinking to return the next day and retrieve it. Most of its goods had been emptied anyway, onto the head of Balak. The mood, though somber to say the least, did not stop Ishtob from smiling at the thought of seeing Balak on all fours scurrying away. He looked down at Jezreel as though together they had put the devil himself to flight. "We sent that slimy weasel running for his life didn't we little man?"

It only took seconds for his mind to return to the task at hand, the task of how to make known to Hosea what he had witnessed and of presenting Jezreel safe and sound back to his father.

Ishtob and Jezreel arrived at the home of Hosea and found him sitting in the courtyard. When Hosea saw them approaching and realized that it was his own son Jezreel in the arms of his lifelong friend, he quickly leaped to his feet, and ran to meet them. As soon as he reached them, Hosea snatched Jezreel from Ishtob's arms, and in a panic began to ask questions.

"Why do you have my son? Where is Gomer? Has harm befallen her?" Hosea wailed! Ishtob watched as Hosea carefully examined the baby's every limb to make sure his little body was in perfect order. When Hosea was convinced the baby was unimpaired, he turned his attention once again to Ishtob. With a look as sad and forlorn as Ishtob had ever seen in his life Hosea asked once more, "Where is my wife, what has happened to her?"

Ishtob attempted to gain the strength he needed to speak, but the words evaded him. Instead, he placed his hand on the shoulder of Hosea and gently began to lead him back into the courtyard. Quietly they walked, as though the weight of the world was upon both of them. Hosea's steps were labored, because fear and dread made his legs weak.

Ishtob motioned for Hosea to sit down at the wooden table in the center of the courtyard, while he paced nervously back and forth. Then he took a long breath and began to speak. "There is no easy way for me to tell you this, my friend, but today I found Gomer in the act of adultery." Hosea peered toward his friend in confusion as his heart sank within him. He sat in complete silence, trying to take in the words he had heard. He shook his head in disbelief as numbness flooded his soul. "I would rather have heard that some beast had devoured her." He said, while looking away out into the emptiness of the air.

"Where and how did you find her?" Hosea questioned. His eyes were strongly fixed on Ishtob and it seemed he could look right through him. "You know that I have been out looking everywhere for her. Many days I have not rested as my heart ached to find her. Are you sure Ishtob? Please tell me this is not true!"

Ishtob's sorrowful expression told Hosea that the terrible news was true. After allowing the reality of Gomer's betrayal to sink in, Hosea slammed his fist against the table in frustration. Ishtob stopped pacing and sat down across from him. "I want to speak to you with openness," Ishtob said, looking straight into Hosea's eyes. "Truth and knowing, as hard as that is, can be dealt with." Hosea listened carefully to his dear friend as Ishtob continued. "It is the unknown which eats at a man, like a sickness that devours his flesh. So, I am going to tell you everything I know. I found her with the man called Balak. They were at the entrance to the city, and I was carrying away the spoiled fruit of the day. I happened upon them and beheld them sealing their affection with a kiss. When I had made my presence known to them, Balak fled like a scared animal. He left her to fend for herself Hosea! It was then she began to beg for mercy and to ask me to bring the baby to you! She said she could not cause you to lose both her and the baby. And..." Ishtob looked down at the ground in his own disbelief of what he would say next. "And, she asked me to tell you that she loved you, and was so sorry for hurting you!"

Hosea pulled Jezreel tight against his chest and never said a word as he began to rock back and forth. The words Ishtob had just spoken stabbed at his heart, cutting deep wounds of anguish. With one strong hand Hosea held onto his son, and with the other he began to rend his own clothes. He tore at them while wailing and sobbing loudly. Finally his grief overtook him and sent him to his knees. The impact caused the dust to fly into the air as his body plunged to the ground with a sickening thud. Hosea's hand found its way to the dirt, and brought a fist full of ashes to cast upon his head. Part of the dust fell upon Jezreel, making him cry out. The baby's arms and legs were flinging about wildly.

Ishtob watched them both, and considered reaching down to take the baby out of the arms of his father. Instead he reasoned, "It was only proper that Jezreel lament, and mourn the sins of his mother likewise." So he let them both weep.

With every tear that fell, Hosea chastened himself for ever taking Gomer to be his wife in the first place. His words began to pour out in anger;

"She is no longer my wife,
and I am not her husband.
Let her remove the adulterous look from her face
and the unfaithfulness from between her breasts.
Otherwise I will strip her naked
and make her as bare as on the day she was born!
I will make her life like a desert, and
I will turn her soul into a parched land!
May she die from thirst!
She said, 'I will go after my lovers,
who give me my food and my water,
my wool and my linen, my olive oil and my drink.'
Therefore I will block her path with thornbushes;
I will wall her in so that she cannot find her way.
I will expose her lewdness
before the eyes of her lovers.
No one will take her out of my hands."

Hosea finished speaking and moaning the awful sounds of grief. He knew deep within his heart this was just hurt talking. Even now in the deep recesses of his soul he knew that he still loved her. He had loved her from the first time he ever set eyes on her. He also knew that deep hurts can either make a man bitter or better. Hosea could never allow bitterness to rule within his heart.

So he allowed the anger to be transformed into determination. He knew he must set his heart to overcome this, and to protect Jezreel, in every way possible.

Throughout the night his sleep was restless as his spirit was driven toward her, as it had been the very first evening when he found her so long ago. In his dreams he could see himself going out into the night and finding her, then lovingly bringing her home.

When the long awaited morning finally broke, Hosea awoke with a deep sickening feeling within his stomach. Oh how he wished the events from yesterday were only a dream. But when he saw Jezreel lay without his mother, Hosea knew that it was all too real. As he lay beside his son, he quietly began to pray. "Lord, hear the prayer of your servant Hosea, please give me wisdom and strength. Wherever Gomer is this morning, please speak deeply into her soul. Lead her back to me. I still love her, and I will never let her go from my heart."

Hosea's prayer was interrupted by a light knock on the door. He quietly went to the door to see who it was. As the door opened, Hosea peered out to find Ishtob standing in the light of dawn. A lady was with him, someone Hosea had never seen before. Ishtob spoke softly so as not to awaken anyone else. "I hope you won't mind, but I have brought Melea; she is a wet nurse for the baby." Hosea tried to comprehend what his friend had just said. "A wet nurse?" He asked. Ishtob gave a quick glance toward where Jezreel was lying. "Yes Hosea, a wet nurse, for the baby to take milk!"

Hosea's mind had been far too consumed with grief to have given any consideration to the need. As the realization set in of how many hours had passed since the baby had nursed, Hosea knew it was the hand of God which had sustained Jezreel. The baby had slept all night with hardly a whimper. As the three of them stood in the doorway however, and almost as though the baby understood the provision now made for him, he began to cry.

Hosea realized the kindness and generosity of Ishtob to arrange for this, so with a grateful heart he motioned for Melea to enter. He thanked Ishtob profusely for his thoughtfulness. Hosea, as a prophet, had always given himself to the care and provision of others. And while it felt strange and awkward for him to suddenly be on the receiving end of kindness, it also brought him great comfort.

Melea went about taking care of Jezreel, while Ishtob and Hosea sat in the courtyard, sipping hot tea. Even though it was morning, both men were exhausted from the fitful night of worry and contemplation. The warmth from the tea brought some comfort to Hosea. He sat with his elbows resting heavily upon the table. His hair was a mess, his eyes were bloodshot, and his face bore the pain that comes from losing one's wife.

Both men sat in the courtyard for many hours in a forlorn state of mind. Hosea stroked at his beard thoughtfully, while Ishtob's eyes slowly opened and shut, opened and shut, the result of fatigue. Hosea finally placed his big hands on the top of the table and sluggishly pushed himself up from his sitting position. Ishtob opened his drowsy eyes slightly and watched Hosea walk a few steps away from the table. Hosea's back was now to his caring friend and his voice startled Ishtob as he began to speak, partly to himself and partly to Ishtob.

"I cannot turn her over to the authorities, for they would surely have her stoned to death." He turned back to face Ishtob as he continued. "You know that without any doubt they would love to release all their fury on her. I will not allow it! My heart will not permit it." Hosea walked back and stood in front of Ishtob, who was now more awake due to Hosea's words. But it was Hosea's next movement which completely jolted Ishtob to full alertness. Hosea slowly leaned over and placed his hands on Ishtobs shoulders, so that only a few inches separated their faces. No longer did Hosea's expression show defeat, but instead, a stern visage of resolve. "I will find her, and I will show forth my love for her. Even now while she is with Balak, I will provide for her, and I will protect her without her even knowing it. Whatever I must do to bring her back to me, this is what I will do. I will never forsake her!"

Ishtob's eyes widened at the bold, unyielding proclamation made by Hosea. But nothing could have prepared him for the words Hosea spoke next. "Will you help me Ishtob, will you please help me find my wife, and bring her back home?"

Ishtob wasn't sure how to respond! Although the words from Hosea sounded so strong and hopeful, he knew it would be an almost impossible task to carry out. His dutiful service in finding a wet nurse for an innocent baby was one thing, but to involve himself in the restoration of an adulterous woman was another! Not only could Ishtob feel the weight of Hosea's body leaning on his shoulders, but also the weight of what it means to join in a covenant of reconciliation.

After considering the matter and concluding that he was already deeply committed, Ishtob answered. "Yes, Hosea I will help you! I will do everything I can to help you find her and to bring her home. But you must understand; I am not doing this because she deserves it. Instead, I am doing it because your love for her is beyond anything I have ever witnessed."

So that morning around the small table in Hosea's courtyard, those two men joined hearts in a covenant to rescue and save Gomer. Both knew she did not deserve to be saved. Both of them knew she was a woman who was lost in her own desires. But most importantly, both of these men knew the power of grace and love! It would be the innocent seeking and saving the guilty. It was salvation's glorious plan!

Chapter 15

What My Soul Lusted After Brought Nothing But Emptiness!

"The payment for sin is death; but God's gift is eternal life, provided by Jesus Christ our Lord."

Romans 6:23

"... The way of sinners is a difficult path."

Proverbs 13:15

Gomer awoke at the vineyard of her mother with the strong arms of Balak wrapped tightly around her. The smell of blossoms from the trees in the vineyard slipped in through the small windows and filled her senses. Balak's body lay hot against her, but she did not dare move, less she wake him. All she wanted to do was quietly lay there and try to make some sense of her own actions and deeds.

Since arriving at the vineyard many days ago she had not stopped from tireless labor. Gomer slowly moved

her hand in front of her face to examine it. It showed all
the signs of the vineyard's toil. Her hands were laced with
cuts and bruises from countless days of tending her
mother's vineyard. The labor caused her muscles to ache.
But the ache in her arms and back could not compare
with the deep lonely ache within her heart. A tear slipped
down the side of her face, dripping onto the white soft
fabric she lay on. Her mind flew across the mountain,
back to Hosea and her little son Jezreel. Oh how she
missed her baby so!

"*Momma still loves you,*" she whispered in her mind.
Gomer took a long and cleansing breath, "*If things could only
have been different*", she pondered, "*but isn't that the excuse I
have been using for most of my life?*" She reached down and
clinched the covers, pulling them tight under her chin,
perhaps to offer a small bit of comfort against her warring
soul.

Her movement had awakened Balak, and he turned
on his back while reaching his arms high above his head
to stretch every fiber of his strong body. Gomer lay still,
hoping he would drift back to sleep, but he did not.
Instead, his hand found its way to her side, and with a
playful slap he tapped her. "So what shall we eat for the
morning meal?" He asked. "Our passion last night has left
my stomach very hungry and empty."

Gomer sat up, placing her feet on the cool floor,
with her back to Balak. The white cloth of her night gown
showed the arch of her back. "I will go and find wood for
the morning fire, then prepare your meal." She got up and
left the room, leaving Balak still half asleep. As she passed
through the doorway he called out to her in a slumberous

tone, "just come and get me when it is ready, my beautiful servant girl!"

The air outside was cool as she stepped into the courtyard. She took water from a pitcher and poured it into a basin and slowly cupped her hands as she dipped them into the refreshing water. As she brought it to her face, its coldness awakened her senses and instantly she became aware of everything around her. A puzzled look crossed her face as the smell of smoke now invaded her mind. She stood there for a brief moment attempting to determine where the odor was coming from. She peered out to look beyond the front wall and there she could see it; smoke was rising just on the other side of the wall. She had not noticed it before, but now she was wide awake, and she knew her eyes were not deceiving her.

Gomer walked slowly to the doorway of the courtyard. *"Could there be someone out there,"* she thought to herself. *"Someone who might cause me harm?"* To most women this fear would have sent them rushing back into the house, but not Gomer. She had been fighting all her life, and one more encounter with the unknown mattered little to her. She carefully peered around the corner of the doorway and could not believe her eyes. A fire had already been built, with wood piled all around, and that wasn't all. Pressed up against the wall was a table with fruits and breads, meats and vegetables, all assembled neatly and rounded to perfection. Gomer was now more puzzled than ever. "Who could have done this?" She asked out loud.

She walked over to the table and ran her fingers along the edge, pondering the blessing that had been brought to her. She carefully walked beyond the boundaries of the fire's warmth and gazed out in every direction to see if she might catch but a glimpse of this secret benefactor. Still, only emptiness lay out in front of her; there was no sign of who had come her way. All she could reason was that a power greater than herself was surely watching over her.

"My, my, you must work with the swiftness of a magician," Balak said, as he now stood in the doorway of the courtyard. Gomer whirled about quickly, "you shouldn't sneak up on a woman like that," she said, while running her fingers through her hair as though straightening it, trying to gather her composure.

She approached the table and began to fumble through the food in an attempt to prepare a meal for Balak. "Where did all this food come from, have you been hiding it from me?" He asked. Before she could respond Balak started in again. "Aw, I understand, you have set out to prepare a meal fit for a king such as myself. And I shall be served by the most beautiful servant girl in all the land. You must surely love me to honor me in such a grand fashion."

As Balak talked on and on, basking in his vain glory, Gomer spoke nothing. Instead, she continued to labor, preparing the meal. Balak sat down, never taking his eyes off her. He picked up a small stick of wood and tossed it onto the fire. "Now my love, you could at least speak to your prince. Is this glorious feast being prepared in celebration of the passion that we shared last night?"

His resistance grew thin and he couldn't sit for
long; her white gown revealing beautiful olive skin, and
tempting him more. He gently moved in behind her while
running his hands down her arms, as he kissed the back of
her neck. Gomer stood stiff, and flinched at the touch of
his lips to her skin. Balak whispered closely from behind
her, "My little servant girl, how thankful you must be to
finally have a real man in your life, one who can ignite the
fires of passion within your flesh."

Gomer turned about, looking eye to eye with him.
"Now you listen to me, I am not your servant girl, and the
only fire of passion which burns in my flesh is the desire
to vomit because of your egotistical attitude. And as far as
this meal is concerned, all I can tell you is the God of
Israel must surely be watching over me. And even though
I have strayed from Him, His love has somehow found its
way to me."

Balak gave a very displeasing look at her, "I never
thought I would see the day when talk of God would
come from your lips. You have changed; I do believe that
man Hosea has bewitched you! But just in case you have
forgotten, I know who you are, and you are nothing but a
self-righteous prostitute!"

Gomer was furious as she ripped free from Balak's
stare and ran back into the house. He stood for a brief
moment, shaking his head in disgust, and then let out a
laugh that chased Gomer like an eerie shadow, all the way
into the house. "Just let the God of Israel try and snatch
you away from me," he shouted, mocking her very soul.

Balak went about murmuring to himself. "God of
Israel, bah, I am not afraid of this God. There is not a

stronger man in all Israel than I, and it seems to me this
God has failed in his watchful duties, seeing how he has
allowed Gomer to slip back into my hands." Balak let out
another roar of laughter as he sat down by the fire and
began to eat the morning meal.

By mid afternoon Gomer was back in the vineyard
attempting to harvest more of the meager figs hanging
from the branches. The lack of rainfall had yielded only
one harvest that year, and the income was scarce. Gomer
despairingly searched each of the gnarled branches in the
hope of finding just one more precious fig to add to the
harvest. She carefully dropped the gathered crop into the
basket and examined the yield; it was a scant result. From
all her labor and toil, most of what she gained was a deep
unending ache in her hands and arms. She picked up a fig
from the basket and dusted it off with her apron. Bringing
it to her lips, she partook of the fruit's sweetness. "If only
my mother could be here to teach me how to better care
for this place." she said.

Gomer wiped the juice from her lips as she sat
down under one of the trees. She leaned back against its
trunk as a cool refreshing breeze rippled through her hair
and tossed it about gently. She crossed her feet and placed
a hand full of figs in her lap. One by one she nibbled at
them, while talking out loud to anyone who would listen.
"Mother, I am doing the best I can. The crop has been
small, and there is no one willing to help me. Remember
mother, when you were nearing your last breath and I told
you about a man that I loved? Well I have hurt him! It is
the one thing I seem to do best in life, hurt other people! I

have hurt him by allowing myself to be seduced by a man who is cruel, and heartless." Gomer shook her head in disbelief at her own actions. "What a fool I have been! Yet somehow, even when people know what is right, they still do foolish things."

Gomer leaned over and picked a blade of grass, allowing it lay in her hand. The wind quickly picked it up and carried it away. "Why can't my troubles be carried away that easily?"

She was startled by the loud and boisterous voice of Balak, as he interrupted her thoughts. "Then you better start praying that your God sends a whirlwind, because you are about to have more trouble than you can imagine." Balak walked between the rows of trees toward her.

Gomer jumped to her feet, fearing he had heard all the things she had spoken. As Balak approached, Gomer could see that he wasn't alone; another man was with him, one of elder years. The man's face seemed familiar to Gomer as she studied him. He had the appearance of a man with great means; very wealthy. His clothing was brightly colored, and his hair and beard were neatly groomed. He was carrying a document, and both men's faces bore signs of deep sincerity.

"Gomer, this is Achaz. He desires to speak with you about a debt your mother owed on this vineyard." Balak said! And once again he turned and left her alone to fend for herself. The sweetness of the fruit Gomer had just tasted now seemed bitter. She remained by the basket, awaiting the man to make the full length of the row. When he arrived, he peered in the bushel, as though taking account of the harvest. As he examined the baskets contents, his fingers thoughtfully pinched at his lips. He began to speak with great authority; you would have thought he owned the entire world!

"Gomer, you may not remember me, but how well my heart reckons of you. You were but a small girl, playing here in this very orchard the last time I saw you. It was the day your mother contracted a debt upon this land, a debt to provide the means with which she would run this business. That was many years ago, and she always paid ...without fail, until"..., and then he stopped, to give what seemed to be some reverence to Diblaim. But the small regard he showed only lasted for a few seconds. Achaz arrogantly took a fig from Gomer's hand and began to nibble at it while he spoke. "Your mother paid without fail until she became sick and nigh unto death. Since that time the debt has gone unpaid."

Both stood for what seemed like an eternity examining each other. It was as if two old warriors were assessing the enemy before going to battle. Gomer knew the weight and power in the words Achaz had spoken, for she had witnessed many souls lost into the pains of slavery through unpaid debts. Her world of promiscuous living had made her an audience far too many times to the stage of human suffering. All at the hands of men who valued land and soil far more than the dignity of the human spirit.

She could feel a raging anger begin to rise up within her. "Why have you come telling me this now? For I have spent many days tending this vineyard, and I alone am the sole heir to its blessings." Fear arose within her, making her close her eyes. She knew the price an unpaid debt could bring. She slowly opened her eyes once more and looked around at all the trees and vines hanging empty, empty of any means of redemption. She spoke again, this time speaking to the vineyard itself. "Am I not only an heir to your blessings, but perhaps now, an heir to your curse as well?"

Achaz cleared his throat before speaking, he knew the words he was about to say would shackle Gomer, with chains of slavery if she could not pay the debt. "From the looks of the harvest it seems impossible for you to clear this debt," he said, peering one last time into the basket. "Do you have any means by which you can pay this obligation?"

Gomer poised herself with the boldness of a tigress backed into a corner. "As you can well see, the crop has been little, and I have hardly enough to feed my own household. How can I clear this debt of which you speak? But if you could give me one more harvest, I will surely pay you all that is owed."

Achaz walked over and picked up the basket as though it had just become his own. "You know I cannot do that. I have already given ample time for you to mourn the loss of your mother, and time for you to make some payment. Now I am here to claim my entitlement." He continued talking as he walked from vine to vine occasionally finding a shriveled fig here and there, dropping it disgustingly into the basket. Then he began to speak words that confused Gomer's mind. "Had it not been for your lover, I am sure I would have lost you, lost you forever! Yes, without his help in seducing you here, I would never have been able to bring you into my house as a servant to pay this debt."

Gomer was now step by step with him, inquisitive as to what he meant by his confusing statement. The revelation of betrayal caused her to seethe in hot boiling anger. "What do you mean, had it not been for my lover? Who are you talking about? I demand that you tell me at once! Who helped you by seducing me to become a servant into your house?"

Achaz continued through the vineyard, now amused by her sudden interest in his extravagant plot. "Now, now my child, servant- hood is not such a terrible thing." He tried to calm her defiant spirit, but it would not be calmed! Instead, her heart was racing within her, pounding like the sound of many horses' feet coming to take her away. "No! I will not calm down, nor will my spirit be at ease until you tell me of whom you speak, and if not, then I will end your life here and now!" Her sweaty palms defiantly clutched the garden hoe that rested in her hands.

Achaz was taken aback by her fiery nature, and he couldn't help but give out a small chuckle, even though his own life had now been threatened. "My beautiful little servant girl," he said, while wrestling the hoe from her hands. "Just calm down and I will tell thee of my cunning plan to capture you, and to bring you into my household. There was another who also owed me a great debt; your lover, the man called Balak. He too would have been my servant, but he offered me a deal. He promised to give to me a jeweled treasure, a little servant girl along with her mother's vineyard."

Achaz let out a chuckle and shook his head in delight. "Oh he is a crafty one, bargaining with me, and boasting how he could lure you here with enticing words and cause you to sell your very soul. Now, I shall pay him handsomely with his freedom, for you are worth far more to me! Not only will I have your mother's vineyard, but I will have you to bring me pleasure for many days! You see, Balak is like a serpent, used to beguile you that I might own you, soul and body."

Gomer fell to the earth, her body becoming one with the dirt. Tears of betrayal poured from her eyes. She cursed Balak, and pounded her fist into the earth. She cursed herself, and the day she was born. Anger poured forth once again for her mother, attempting to blame anyone, and everyone for her own dilemma. "My spirit is dying within me," she lamented. "What my soul lusted after has brought me nothing but emptiness! What my eyes looked upon has made me blind, naked, and miserable!"

In her dismay she had failed to notice the crowd of very large men approaching her. They lifted her from the earth violently, Gomer kicking and screaming the whole time. One of the men pulled her hands unmercifully behind her back and tied them with roping. The others knelt in front of her, placing chains between her feet. Seeing an opportunity to take revenge, Gomer kicked one assailant in the face, delivering him promptly on his back. He sat up as Gomer looked him over; confident she had inflicted great pain. Blood was dripping from the side of his mouth, and he slowly wiped it off with the back of his hand. "You dirty filthy whore," he ranted at her, "I'll make you pay for this." He got up and slapped her, again and again, as an onslaught of his fury was unleashed. Her vision became cloudy and with every traumatic blow the vineyard and her surroundings faded to black. She lay silent and still, breathing only shallow; breaths! It was the voice of Achaz which brought her back to consciousness. "Enough!" she heard him say, as the men lifted her up once more. The taste of blood filled her mouth, and her stomach burned with pain!

She was led away, with chains between her feet and with every step the metal cut deep into her flesh. They led her off the brow of the hill where the vineyard sat tucked in behind the house. She was too numb to cry! But her recent tears were mixed with mud and stung at her eyes as she walked. They were soon in front of the courtyard where just that morning a blessing of food had been delivered. That was the only good thing that entered her mind. Strangely, even under these circumstances she wondered once more where the blessing had come from.

The smoke from the fire was still ascending up into the sky as they rounded the corner of the yard. She turned her head slightly, to see Balak still tending the fire. She began to scream at him; "may God cause your soul to burn in hell!" she lashed out. Balak picked up a rag, then walked over to where she was and forcefully formed a gag. He stood smiling at her with an evil and wicked grin. Without mercy he spat in her face! "Thank you for the passion and pleasure you have brought to me my servant girl," he said with a taunting wink of the eye.

Even though her voice had been silenced, her eyes burned with despise. Balak turned to walk away. "You're not worth killing!"... But before he could insult her any more, Achaz interrupted him! "Better a live servant than a dead whore," he said, as he motioned for them to lead her away.

Gomer was brought to the house of Achaz to serve him in all manners of slavery. There were long days tending to crops in the fields and longer nights while her body was savagely used for the pleasure of many men. Oh how violent the wages of sin! Oh how dreadful the penance of disobedience!

Chapter 16

Prisoners' Chains and Bleeding Stripes

"For the kind of brokenness God wants us to experience sets us free from sin and provides salvation. We never regret spiritual brokenness..."

2 Corinthians 7:10

The house of Achaz set just north of Jerusalem in the once bustling city of Gibeah. During the reign of King Saul it had served as host to one of the royal residences of Israel. But that was long ago, in another day and time. All the shadows of Gibeah's past grandeur had faded with the passing years. If there was any glimmer of beauty left in this city, it was in the sprawling residence owned by the cruel master, Achez. The outward appearance of this mountain vista with ornate rock walls was pristine; yet, the interior was filled with an assemblage of lost souls.

Day after day Gomer watched the horde of bondservants surrounding her, grow weaker and weaker.

Their bodies were beaten down by laborious toil. The small portions of food received each day did little to strengthen them against the continuous assault to the body and soul. It didn't take long, even as strong willed as Gomer was, for her own body to wane away. But it was her spirit which suffered gravely, and it was the dark of night which haunted her most, with memories of what life could have been. In these dark hours there were many voices which spoke into her mind. They pushed her down – down, into the strong holds of despair.

Occasionally, Hosea's face appeared to her in visions, and the cry of Jezreel would echo in her ears, awaking her from agonizing sleep. She would wrestle her body to respond, to get up and speak to Hosea, to beg him to come and rescue her. Then at other times she would cradle her arms, as if holding Jezreel. But when she awoke, it was always the same. Hosea and Jezreel had only been empty visions in her hopeless dreams.

On one of these nights she was allowed to leave the slave house and walk out into the fields surrounding the house of Achaz. As she moved higher up the gentle hillside, she peered into the night sky. It was littered with a million stars, brightly shinning their affection down upon her abandoned and lost soul.

By the soft glow of the full moon she could see the great cedar trees swaying in the light breeze. Gomer found a clearing and lay down in the tall plush grass. Her bones and muscles throbbed without mercy; a constant reminder of the sinful choices she had made. As she lay there, a faint tear slipped down her cheek. Looking into the sky she was reminded of the night when she and Hosea had went up on the rooftop and the rain had begun to fall, washing away the bitterness between them. "God," she began to pray softly, "please let it rain tonight. Let me feel your mighty fingers once more in the droplets of rain, that my sins may be washed away."

She paused a moment and listened to the silence surrounding her. It was as though she expected an angel to suddenly appear and save her from this life of torment. But as the minutes passed by and no angelic deliverer came, her own voice began to penetrate the darkness.

"GOD, where are you?" She yelled! "Can you even hear me? Do you even care that I am dying in my sin?" She waited again for a divine response, but there was none! Only the heavy condemnation of her own choices spoke back to her. As the hours passed and she considered her life, it became more and more clear to her that there was no one else to blame, other than herself. And this acceptance of responsibility for her own deeds was the first step toward freedom! She continued to lay there, with her eyes heavenward, and lowered her voice with a reverenced tone, praying once more.

"Please God, save me from my iniquity. I have cast away my life; I have thrown away your great mercy. When you provided for me a grand deliverer, a savior, I wasted his love. I do not deserve your mercy, or your tender compassion. But you, oh God, are the only hope I have. Without you, my life will end in destruction. Forgive my sin, and take me back! Lead me once more into the arms of love; the arms my spirit longs for!"

She prayed long into the night until she finally drifted off to sleep. Toward morning she was awakened by some commotion around her. She thought she heard someone walking nearby. She sat up and scanned the field around her in the dim morning light. Everything seemed fresh, and renewed. And strangely, even her own soul felt this way! She shivered in the coolness of the damp air, and pulled her cloak tight around her body for warmth.

"Is anyone out there?" she called. *Perhaps it was a wild beast which stalked her, and its motion had jolted her from sleep*, she considered. "Tell me, who you are, if anyone is there?" She called out once more.

When no one answered, she arose slowly, still ever so watchful. "The sun will rise soon," she whispered to herself, "I must get back before Achaz calls for me." Cautiously, Gomer began to walk the path leading back to her house of slavery. She had not walked far until something caught her eye. Whatever it was, rested just ahead of her on the very path she had traveled the evening before. When only a few paces separated her from the object, she was able to tell that it was a sack. It seemed to have been placed there deliberately, perhaps so she would find it. "*Could it have purposely been left here by who ever had startled me from sleep only moments before,*" she wondered?

Gomer stooped down, but with vigil awareness. "Come out and show yourself," she called. "I know you are here," she called again. Her eyes darted with apprehension as her fingers, cold and trembling, began to undo the small rope holding the fabric shut. The knot finally came loose, and she gently stretched the top apart, revealing its contents.

She found the sack filled with corn; beautiful corn, ready to bring strength to her weak body. She dug deeper and found a wine skin filled with sweet juices of the vine. She searched again, and excitement grew when she found a smaller bag lying next to the wine skin. She quickly opened it and when she peered inside she could not believe her eyes. A small number of coins were stashed inside. Not just any coins, but fifteen shekels of silver coins was neatly tucked away in the bag.

Suddenly her mind traveled back, back to her life with Hosea. She remembered observing him once while he was writing upon a parchment scroll. This memory stuck with her because she remembered Hosea's reaction to her presence that day. He had quickly rolled up the scroll and tucked it in his belt, embarrassed that she had been able to sneak up on him so easily. But yes, she had seen it, and she never had forgotten the few penned words he had scribed; *"For she did not know that I gave her corn, and wine, and oil, and multiplied her silver and gold...."*

"Could it be?" She thought, as her heart raced within her! She began to frantically scan the fields in every direction, calling out; "Hosea, Hosea, I know you are here somewhere watching over me! Where are you my grand deliverer?" Although Hosea did not appear to her, she was certain his presence was near! She gathered the bag and all its belongings and walked the path back to the house of Achaz, with renewed hope and a cleansed heart!

****

Gomer continued to serve in the house of Achaz for many more days. Early one morning she was jolted awake by a smooth hand that had been placed over her mouth, keeping her from alarming others with a scream. She quickly grabbed at the hand attempting to remove it out of fear, but before she could do so, a sweet and gentle voice spoke to her in a faint whisper. She immediately recognized the voice to be that of a woman named Joanna, also a maidservant.

"Gomer," Joanna spoke in a low soft whisper. "Please listen to me with all your heart, for evil has been planned for you today!" Gomer slowly removed Joanna's hand, and in the faint light provided by the morning moon, their eyes met in trust and full attention. "What is wrong Joanna, what message is this that you bring to me?"

Both women had grown to trust one another soul to soul since arriving at the house of Achaz. Joanna was beautiful and radiant, with dark green eyes that could melt any heart which came into their vision. She had often represented the grace of God to the downcast spirit of Gomer. Every day Joanna encouraged her, and spoke to Gomer rich words, filled with hope against the hardness of servant-hood.

Others in the great room of servants were becoming restless because of the whispers of the two women. "Get up and come with me, I have something very important to tell you," Joanna bid her.

Gomer quietly rolled to her side and pushed her hands on the dirt flooring to assist herself in standing. The two women carefully stepped between the sleeping bodies of the other women. Gomer pulled her cloak around her shoulders and moved into the early morning air. As they walked, their footsteps disturbed a mother dove and sent her flapping her wings, squawking loudly as she few off. The hand of Joanna was hurriedly tugging Gomer along in nervous apprehension.

Well out of hearing, Joanna stopped and turned to face Gomer. "I regret having startled you awake, but I must inform you of what I learned just last night." "Does it concern me?" Gomer asked in worry. Joanna shook her head in sadness, "yes, it does concern, you." Both women sat on the ground as Joanna began to share the dreaded news.

"Last night I was completing the evening meal in the master's house and I overheard him talking about particular servants that had grown weak and of little worth to him." Gomers heart pounded even harder now in her chest as she listened. "I heard him talking on and on about you Gomer. About how you are growing older and were of little use to him now. And worst of all he talked about how he is going to place you on the servant's block and sell you."

Complete fear raced through Gomer's heart upon hearing these words. But before she could speak a word of terror, Joanna reached forth her hands and tenderly cupped the face of Gomer.

"Listen to me," she entreated Gomer, "my heart is knit with your own. Whether it was providence or the very will of God that brought us together, I will not let you suffer harm." But Gomer interrupted her, as her overwhelming worry began to speak. "What will I do? My body is much too frail to be of any benefit to a new owner!

No one will purchase me, and I shall be left to die at the anger of Achaz when he sees that I bring him no profit."

Joanna slipped her arms around Gomer, embracing her in a deep expression of love as she spoke to her. "From the morning you came bringing gifts of corn to all the servants in the house of Achaz, I have known your heart was good. You risk your own life for all of us. You gave us food from your own possession that we might live. And now I will do all I can to save your life as well."

Both women wept together, shedding many tears of fear and worry. Suddenly Gomer ask, "Did the master speak of when he might bring me to the block, to sell my very soul to death?" Joanna rose from her place and stood as if filled with hurried anxiousness. "Today my dear friend. Achaz has plans to bring you swiftly, before another shekel is put at risk by your weariness."

Gomer felt as though her very spirit would faint within her. She lay over on the ground relinquishing her soul to defeat. "My heart will burst within me," she lamented. "I thought I had within my bosom a promise, given to me by Hosea, and the God of Israel. It was a promise my faith had embraced! I actually believed that I would be saved from this hell which engulfs me. How can I believe now? How is it that I can trust, when the road ahead shows nothing but complete darkness?"

Joanna knelt beside her. "Shhh, stop your weeping my friend, for God this night has brought into my heart a plan, a plan to deliver you." Gomer sat upright, attempting to brush her hair away from her tear covered face. "What is this plan that God has brought into your heart? Tell me please that my soul may live!"

The hand of Joanna wiped away the tears from Gomer's eyes. "I myself shall escape in this very hour! I will go and find the man you love! I will tell him of your great dilemma, and plead with him that he might buy you for himself."

Gomer shook her head, "No, you must not, lest your own life be taken by the master for escaping his hand of ownership." But Joanna would not be quieted. "What is my life? If it had not been for you and the secret gift of corn brought from the sack, I am sure my life would have been sniffed out long ago."

"But what if Hosea will not have me back?" Gomer asked! "I know my wickedness has caused him great sorrow! He must surely despise me." Joanna positioned herself on her knees in eager response. "Has your soul forgotten the coins, and the food? How can you doubt the ever present help that looked after you? You must believe with all your heart, now more than ever, that it was Hosea who watched over you. Even when your soul had sinned, it surely was He that brought you food and wine, and the coins."

Suddenly a look of joyful realization exploded on the faces of both women as they shouted their revelation in unison. "The coins!" They both said. "Those blessed coins." Joanna's excitement grew as she now commanded Gomer as if she had just became her guardian angel. "I will take the coins to Hosea as proof that I have been with you, and, that what I tell him concerning you being sold is true!"

Both sat for a brief moment, as they considered their plan. Then complete joy overtook them and they leaped into one another's arms in a hearty embrace. They held each other while rocking back and forth, basking in the marvelous scheme arranged between them. But Joanna, remembered the urgency of the hour. "Oh stop this silly rejoicing; we have no time for this! Hurry now, go and get the coins, and then you must tell me where I might find this grand deliverer of yours."

It seemed like an eternity before Gomer arrived back with the coins in hand. She sat down in front of Joanna and gently held out her hand. Joanna could see that Gomer had placed the coins back into the small bag in which she had found them. She had carefully tied the rope in the same fashion around the top. Gomer gave the bag to Joanna. "He knew what he was doing all the time didn't he?" Gomer said. Joanna closed her hand tight around the bag. "Yes he did, and I am going to believe with all my heart that even now he will not fail you."

"Please be careful! I pray that God will bestow many blessings on you for this love you are showing me," Gomer said. Joanna now stood, looking like a beautiful princess going off to conquer all the armies of the world. "The same God who watches over you, will guide my every footstep," she said, reaching down to touch the face of Gomer.

Gomer told her where to find Hosea, and then kissed the side of Joanna's face. "The sun is rising, you must be going. I shall pray for you every moment." She paused, looking back into the eyes of Joanna. "And please, tell Hosea that I love him, more than life itself, I love him." Joanna gave a wink of the eye and smiled, "I shall carry your message with faith and assurance!" With that she turned and quickly ran away.

Gomer walked back to the servant's house, praying for Joanna as she went. When she arrived back, she was met by Achaz, standing with his hands perched on his sides. "Where have you been, you filthy whore?" he said angrily. Gomer opened her mouth to speak but before she could do so Achaz instructed her to prepare to leave. "You are not going to work in the fields today, but instead you shall be sold! Gather your belongings, for by this evening you will be the property of another."

His words had been cold and without any consideration of her own feelings. Like an animal or an object made of wood or stone, Gomer would be sold to the highest bidder. She solemnly went inside the meager servant's quarters to retrieve the few items she called her own. As she worked, placing the belongings in a bag, the other servants hardly even looked her way. Not one of them came over to bid her good bye, and no one embraced her.

Gomer walked out the doorway, speaking in her own heart to the audience of her mind. "*We have been reduced to less than human,*" she said. "*Not one here in this house is left with even the will to share another's burden. There is no feeling left, and no caring spirit! It has all been removed by the whip of oppression.*"

As she made her way into the courtyard, she saw other women emerging from the houses nearby. They too were carrying what seemed to be their own belongings, gathered for a journey. She would not be alone in her walk to the auction block. Not a single one spoke to the other; but instead, each woman was lost in her own thoughts and concerns.

Gomer quickly scanned the group to compare her worth against those standing around her. Each woman looked as if death itself would be the next companion to take their hand and lead them away. Even at this assumption Gomer still felt the other women gathered were in better condition than she was.

She walked over and sat down on a low wall surrounding their confinement and waited. The rising sun gently peeked over the trees and warmed her face as it touched her skin. She took a strand of her hair and pulled it out in front of her face to examine it. She brought it just under her nose and smelled of it. It bore the odor of sweat and labor; that of a woman who had lost all dignity. Her fingers gently twisted the black lock allowing strand by strand to fall from her grip. Then her mind went to Joanna. Had she been able to escape the compound without being caught? Would she be able to find Hosea and share her dreaded plight?

Once again she closed her eyes, softly praying for Joanna. As the moments passed, the sun rose higher in the eastern sky and now became hot on her skin. And with each passing second she knew that Joanna could be that much closer to finding Hosea.

Footsteps coming from her right brought her mind and eyes open once again. "Alright you treacherous whores, the time has come for you bring the master a profit," one of them said. There were three men now inside the area of their confinement and each man was carrying chains and fetters. All of the men broke into laughter at the proclamation of profit to be gained from the miserable merchandise set before them.

"Stand up," one of them demanded Gomer. She stood, extending her arms and hands outward as though she had done this many times before. She looked down and watched every motion as the man roughly clamped the wrist fetters tight. She flinched as they pinched at her skin. The fetters were held together by a single chain, with one more attached in the center, serving as the means of leading the captive away. All the other women were shackled in the same manner, none resisting their own fate. They were no longer permitted to sit, but instead were commanded to stand in two rows, facing the opposite line. The men walked around the women, setting a pace between each woman and the other at her side. Although they were standing facing one another, none of them so much as lifted their heads to study the other. Gomer closed her eyes again, and prayed silently, allowing her mind to take her as far from this place as possible.

In but a few moments another commotion brought her back to the present. It was Achaz riding into the courtyard. He rode in between the two lines of women stopping just ahead of them. In between them now lay a huge chain attached to the horse upon which he sat. Gomer could not take her eyes off that horse. It was the same horse Balak had used to entice her. There Tryphon stood; his white muscular body radiant in the brilliant morning light. Knowing that it would be Tryphon which lead her away to the auction block only deepened the overwhelming sense of betrayal.

Soon the men began to walk to each woman while attaching the center chain between the fetters, to the weighty chain lying on the ground between them. The center chain wasn't long enough to allow them to stand completely upright, so their backs were slightly bent. After all was complete, each woman stood silently, waiting the moment when Tryphon would step forward, leading them away to their next destiny.

Chapter 17

A Ransom Paid in Full

"So I redeemed her for fifteen shekels of silver and five
bushels of barley and a measure of wine."

Hosea 3:2

"You also, have been paid for, at a great price..."

1 Corinthians 6:20

Achaz sat atop Tryphon for what seemed like an
eternity, all the while giving orders to the men gathered
around. He instructed them concerning the work of the
day, and called out different servants to be assigned to
particular fields or some labor within the household.
Gomer and the five other women stood bent over, their
backs aching from the awkward position. They listened to
Achaz, all the while knowing the only command given on
this day regarding them, would be to walk the road to the
sale block. Finally, he gave the authoritative charge and
Tryphon immediately responded.

Each woman began to walk, attempting to pace herself with the stallion's steps. They soon discovered that if each of them lifted with all their might, the heavy chain could be raised, enough to allow them to walk more upright. Gomer was set on the left side between two others, one in front and one behind her.

The stony pathway gave little comfort to their already tender feet. They were sore from day after day of heavy labor and long hours of service to their master. Soon, they were moving in a rhythm of expectancy; Tryphon would walk a few steps and then stumble on the uneven paving stones, causing him to jerk forward a bit. With this the hands of each woman would be thrust forward also, causing the metal of the fetters to cut into her flesh. Moans and wails of pain escaped from their lips.

At this moment none of those women could even imagine there was a world beyond their own. The heavy breathing expended while being drug along by the strength of a giant stallion beset them. It confined their minds only to the dusty road under their feet.

As the day wore on and the heat from the midday sun bore down on them, Gomer felt her body becoming weak, and her mind began to spin. It was more and more difficult to keep her balance. Her steps became more labored and awkward which made her legs tremble with frailty. She attempted to control her breathing, and calm herself. She then remembered she had not taken bread all day. Her mind had been too consumed with preparation to even think about it. *"The ration would have been so small it probably would have done little to assist her anyway,"* she thought. Slowly the blackness began to invade the world she wished to remain in. As horrifying as that world was, she fought to remain in its presence. Gomer knew the payment for allowing the blackness to rule her body would send her into a much deeper hell. She groped for light and air, but finally the last glimmer of brightness faded from view.

Gomer stumbled forward, her knees crashing downward to the ground. Immediately her whole body was jerked by a violent force, sending her crashing onto the stony roadway. The intense pulling yanked at her arms, stretching them forward beyond her body, exposing the flesh to the rock and stones in the roadway. The thin fabric of her outer tunic was ripped away and torn, leaving her body barely covered.

A deep stabbing pain raced over her whole body as she began to regain consciousness. Achaz was standing over her, screaming vehemently. "Get up you filthy whore, what is wrong with you?" Gomer attempted to stand by placing her hands on the ground and pushing herself upright. "I am sorry master, I became faint from weakness," she said.

"Look at yourself," Achaz began to rant. "You are covered in dirt and blood, and your garment is torn to shreds. How will I ever sell you now? You worthless creature!" Gomer could not hold back the tears as they came streaming down her face in a river of emotions. But somehow she managed to gather enough strength to speak through her weeping. "I said I am sorry! What more do you want? You have us bound like animals Achaz! Is there not one measure of compassion left in your heart? I have served you well, and so have these women here with me, and yet we are no more to you than dung. But do you know something Achaz? I don't hate you; even now I don't hate you. Instead I pray that God will somehow forgive you, because you must be consumed by a deep emptiness inside."

Gomer finished her defense, and stood trembling from fear and pain. But she was glad she had spoken it. Perhaps Achaz would see that she had changed, that something inside of her was different. She bowed her head and waited for the recompense. Achaz said little as he walked back to the side of Tryphon. "If I were to lay my hand on you now, I would only destroy the opportunity to gain any earnings from you. But I will tell you one thing, if you don't sell, I will stone you to death anyway. So let us see who is still alive by tonight!" Achaz mounted Tryphon and commanded him to begin the journey again.

The sun was just beginning to set when they arrived at the place where Gomer would be sold. Many men soon gathered in the cool evening air. All the men sat in rows facing the *bema*, the platform of elevation where each slave would be brought onto for the sale.

Gomer and the other women were attached to wooden post, set along the edges of the assembly, where prospective buyers could inspect each bondservant. Torches which gave a yellow glow were lit and burned all around the congregation. Gomer peered through the shadows cast about, and scanned each face in the crowd to see if she might catch a glimpse of Hosea. But her heart was left empty, for he was not to be found. "He must come," she whispered softly to herself. "Where are you my grand deliverer?"

She began to hear the sounds of bidding as the slaves, one by one, were placed on the sale block. She could hear the sounds of laughter and shouting out bid after bid. The gathering had become festive, as each buyer received the stock they purchased. Gomer stood nearby, shivering in the cool night air as she awaited her turn.

She attempted to wipe away some of the dirt stains from her tunic. She bent down to brush away some of the mire from her feet and legs, when she noticed another set of feet standing in front of her. Gomer lifted her head slowly, to look into the eyes of an elderly woman with the most beautiful smile she had ever seen. The woman lifted a cup filled with the most wonderful, cool, refreshing water Gomer's lips had ever tasted. She did not hesitate as she cupped the vessel with both hands and drank every drop as fast as she could. When she finished, she lowered the cup, and without hesitation the woman filled it once more. Gomer just looked at her and smiled, then consumed the life –giving substance as quickly as her body would allow.

Lowering the cup again she was swept away by a sudden presence, like that of a Spirit, when complete goodness might flood one's soul. Gomer studied the woman now, but not a single word passed between them. But in that brief moment something divine, beyond description, was passed from the angelic woman, straight to the heart of Gomer. Even though the woman had not spoken a word, Gomer suddenly knew that everything was in God's hands, and He would see her through somehow. It was as if life had re-entered Gomer's body.

She desperately wanted to reach out her hand and touch the woman, but there was a radiance surrounding her, one that forbade Gomer from doing so. "Are you an angel? What is your name?" Gomer asked, still studying her with perplexity. The woman opened her mouth, and spoke but one word, "*Erelah,*" for she truly was an angel; a holy messenger sent by God to sustain Gomer in this very hour. Then, like a vapor she vanished, without saying another word, and she was gone. But Gomer felt renewed, strong and alive, for the first time in many, many days. She looked around to see if any of the other slaves along the line had noticed the divine presence. But no one even looked her way. A smile came across her face, but more importantly there was a radiant smile within her heart.

It wasn't but a moment more until she saw Achaz coming toward her. "You are next Gomer. We shall see if death evades you this night." He had actually called her by name. Perhaps the angel *had* restored her humanness and even Achaz was compelled to acknowledge it. He removed the chain holding her to the post and turned to lead her toward the block, but Gomer stood still. The chain tightened, stopping Achaz. He turned to see what was still holding her. "Achaz," she now began to speak to him. "I just want you to know one thing before I go up there on that block. Whether I live tonight by the hand of a buyer, or die at your own hand, I pray God will have His way with you. It is not mine to hate you or even seek revenge. You are now in His hands, and I pray mercy on your soul."

Achaz stood there as though he would speak, like a man weighted down with a thousand millstones of guilt, hung about his neck. His eyes looked so sad, so lost, so defeated. But before he could empty his soul of its heaviness the call came to go to the block. He quietly turned about and led Gomer to the *bema* upon which she would stand. Her eyes once more scanned the assembled crowd to see if Hosea could be found among the buyers. Once again however, it was only emptiness which came back to her, for he still wasn't present.

"Who will start the bidding on this dirty ravished excuse for a woman?" The tradesman called out. Gomer heard nothing but laughter roar out from the assembly. Achaz walked over and sat down on the edge of the bema while looking up at Gomer. His eyes still bore the loneliness and emptiness in them that she had witnessed only moments before. Occasionally he glanced in her direction, to see her reaction to the mockery being made at her expense.

For there she stood with her hair matted against her face. Dirt covering her from head to toe mingled with blood from where she had fallen. Who would desire her? For sin had taken a deadly toll. She was the appearance of a life gone array, and the ending result of someone beaten down by sin.

"I will give you one dead swine for her, and that is my final bid," a merchant yelled out through his howling laughter. The whole assembly again burst forth in ridicule. But Gomer was not deterred in her faith! Instead,

she looked straight out into the crowd and never flinched.
Her eyes explored every face for any resemblance of
Hosea.

After a long time, the pretentious bidding came to
an end. No one had bought her, not even a single bid had
been cast in her favor. Everything about Gomer became
frozen in time, and what movement there was, seemed to
be in slow motion. She saw Achaz walking toward her.
He spoke to her, but she did not even hear his words. She
simply watched as once again he took hold of the leading
chain, and began to step from the bema.

From the place where she had been standing in the
center of the sale block, to the first step leading down off
the platform, seemed like a day's journey. Her feet and
legs shifted along, heavy with the weight of knowing her
life would soon end. She made it to the first step and
placed her foot on the splintery surface. Gomer knew she
was descending into a grave of death now. Yet her faith
and trust was still in God. Live or die she would trust
Him. Soon Achaz could strip her of life, as his hatred was
unleashed on her.

But the procession was interrupted. "Wait, wait, I
will buy her. I shall give you fifteen shekels of sliver for
her." Gomer knew the voice well, it was Hosea! Achaz
stopped walking, as Gomer turned to find Hosea in her
vision. He was slightly bent over as though attempting to
catch his breath from a hurried trip. But in Gomer's mind,
he was the most handsome man her eyes could ever have
looked upon.

"Please sir, sell her to me," he said again, still panting for breath. "I will pay you here and now without delay." Gomer was bursting with joy inside, just at the mere sight of Hosea. Her heart welled with emotion at the thought of his act of love.

The assembly had grown quiet and still upon Hosea's bid, and not a man seemed to be moving. Achaz, turned to peer into the crowd to see who this tradesman was that had made such a bid. "Fifteen shekels is but a small price to pay for the very soul of another," he said staring right at Hosea. "Who are you?" Achaz continued, "that you would purchase a woman that is of less value than a dog."

Hosea stepped closer to the bema, and into the light. "I am the Prophet Hosea, and this woman is my wife, having been sold into slavery by her own choices. But please sir, do not keep her from me, for..." he paused, knowing his words would bring scorn from the men gathered around them. "For I love her, I love her with all my heart, and if you will release her to me, then her life will be spared, and you shall have your gain." But Hosea wasn't finished speaking yet! "And sir, you spoke of my offer of fifteen shekels being a small price to pay, well sir, I will give you more." At that moment Gomer saw Ishtob the good market keeper walk out among the crowd. He was pulling a cart laden with bags of corn, just like the one Gomer had discovered in the field so many nights ago. "I will add these five bushels of barley corn and a measure of wine to my bid, Hosea said, now please sir, sell her to me."

The men in the assembly began to whisper among themselves. Others pointed in Hosea's direction making gestures with their hands of unbelief. Hosea slowly extended his own hand toward Achaz. In it lay fifteen shekels of sliver with which he would purchase Gomer. Achaz slowly faced Gomer, looking up at her from just below the bema. In his hand he still held the chain attached to the fetters. His eyes now stared at her, as in deep thought. Little expression showed on his face; only sadness looked out from his eyes. Gomer almost felt sorry for him, for she had never seen a man look so lost in all her life. She watched him, as his body reluctantly turned, "Meet me at the exchange table," he said out into the air.

Achaz began to move with Gomer in tow. They were leaving the bema and headed straight toward the table of purchase. Gomer felt her spirit swell within her, as emotions rose with each step they took. "*I am going home,*" she thought, "*Hosea came to get me! After all I have done he still loves me.*" As they moved toward the table, Gomer noticed that Hosea was walking right in behind them. She glanced over her shoulder and caught eyes with him; she wanted to speak to him, just to say something to him. But what does one say to a man that has just rescued you from the pit of death? Instead, she just smiled at him, a smile that spoke of gratitude. Just his presence so close meant so much to her. She now felt safe, and deeply cared for.

When they arrived at the table, Hosea stepped forward to the side of Achaz. The men conversed with the merchant man sitting behind the table of exchange. Gomer stood behind them only catching a word now and then that passed between them. She listened intently, fearful that something might arise in their dealings which might still prevent the sale. But it was Hosea's voice that captured her mind as the words he spoke overtook Gomer with complete delight. "Paid in full," he said, turning toward Achaz. "Her price is now paid in full, give her to me."

Achaz handed Hosea the lead chain without even looking up at him. He walked away from them; his shoulders hung low in defeat. Hosea moved closer to Gomer and looked at her hands which were still shackled. A sudden realization hit Hosea, and he quickly stepped forward with Gomer in tow, attempting to stop Achaz before he got too far away. Hosea called out to Achaz just as he was preparing to mount Tryphon.

"Achaz, stop, you must give me the keys to the fetters, that I might set Gomer free." Achaz never moved, for he was stunned by what he had just heard. As he faced Hosea, his eyes burned with anger. "She is a whore," Achaz accused. "She has defiled herself with adultery and caused you much disgrace. You cannot just set her free." Hosea placed himself in between Gomer and Achaz. "I can do with her whatsoever my heart desires, for she belongs to me now. I am only going to tell you once more, give me the keys to the fetters, lest I have you brought before the authorities and placed in chains yourself."

Hardly anything moved as both Achaz and Hosea stood eyeing one another. It was the clash between good and evil. The only movement was that of Tryphon who had now become spooked by the tension that filled the air. He thrashed his feet about, moving from side to side, and shaking his head violently.

Hosea simply held out his hand, awaiting the keys, the keys of deaths binding hold, and of the grave's cruel sting. Finally Achaz laid them into Hosea's hand. "There, you can have the keys," he said, "but I am only giving them to you because I must, because I have no choice." Hosea held the keys of freedom in his hand, ready to release Gomer from her prison of wretchedness.

Hosea and Gomer turned and started to walk away. From behind them they could hear Achaz ranting at Tryphon, commanding him to hold still. The sound of a whip filled the air, as he began to beat the stallion, taking all his fury out on him.

Hosea and Gomer had walked but a few paces when Hosea stopped her. He took her hands into his own and gently slipped the key into the lock of the fetter. Click; the sound seemed to echo. Then the other hand, click again, and the chains fell to the ground. Gomer held out her hands. They trembled with both weakness and joy. She looked into the face of Hosea, and fell into his arms. "Thank you my grand deliverer! I am free from death's grip, free from sin's bondage!"

They had embraced but a moment when a terrible commotion erupted from behind them. People were running away from the area where they had left Achaz and Tryphon. The people were screaming in great fear as they quickly moved past them. Hosea and Gomer stood still, letting them pass. When all the crowd had moved beyond them, they saw it; Tryphon had trampled Achaz to death under his feet. It had been a deadly bruise to

Achaz's head that sniffed his life away. And now Tryphon was standing just to the right of where he lay. The stallion's spirit had become calm and peaceful, for the evil one had been defeated.

Chapter 18

Restored to the Fullness of the Kingdom

"My word which I shall speak: it will not return empty, but it will accomplish my perfect will, and have positive results in everything I intend."

Isaiah 55:11

The priests had listened for many days to the address Jezreel had given in defense of his father's writings, and now they sat almost motionless as he concluded the narrative. The weight of responsibility began to show on each of the priests' faces, because soon they would cast lots, and determine the scrolls future.

Jezreel slowly arose and began to walk about the room. While sharing with the priests the final details of the story, he purposefully stopped in front of each of them, addressing them individually. The priest listened intently as Jezreel gave his closing comments.

"You see brethren," he continued, "my father Hosea was an instrument of the Lord. He was used to portray a divine love to all humanity. The day my father bought my mother was a day of propitiation; the paying of a sin debt. After he purchased her and they began to walk the road home, my mother sincerely begged him to allow her to be as one of his servants. 'I am not worthy to be called your wife,' she said. But my father would have nothing of it. 'You will be restored to the fullness of my kingdom,' he told her."

"And so it was, my father brought her home to us, for her to be his beloved wife once more. As I grew into childhood I witnessed my father's love for her. And I witnessed in her a life filled with godliness and holiness. She spoke to me often of how God had changed her, and made her life complete."

"As the days passed little by little her body regained its beauty and health. We were a family again. I spent many days laughing and playing with them. There could not have been a more happy family in all the land of Israel than us."

By now Jezreel had moved to the center of the room as he sat back down on the pillow provided for him. He continued with a sad demeanor. "We were happy, my brethren, until the hatred from our community grew so strong that my father begin to fear for our safety. You see, although my father Hosea had forgiven her, the people it seemed could not. As hard as he tried to convince them she had changed, and that she had found repentance, the people choose condemnation over regeneration."

Jezreel shook his head and ran his fingers through his hair, weary from the pain of remembrance. "It was just like Naomi the midwife had said; 'people are cruel, and while God may forgive a person's sins, the people rarely forget.' The sparks of hatred had fallen within our community and now a raging fire burned out of control. I spent many nights lying close to my father and mother, for fear someone might come and destroy us. For this cause, and my own safety, my father was compelled to send me away."

Jezreel began to weep before the priest. He had not done so until now, but grief and remembrance of those days were so overwhelming, he could not hold it back. His voice was full of sorrow as he continued to speak. "I was ten years old when my father called me in one night and told me that on the morrow I would be sent away. Heartbroken, he told me I would be sent to live with Joanna, the lady who assisted my mother, the day Achaz took her to the block. Thankfully, Joanna had managed to escape on that fateful day, and with the death of Achaz, she too became free. She went to live in the northern providence of our country Israel, and my father thought I would be safe there. The next morning after telling me this, my father and I departed for the house of Joanna, where I lived until I became a man. But I never saw my father Hosea or my mother Gomer ever again. I know not what became of them after that. Some people said a terrible thing befell them, but for all these many years my heart has been left empty without knowing."

Jezreel looked around the room at the priests; the very men he knew would soon decide the fate of the scroll in question. "This, my brethren, is all I know. I have nothing more to share. I have concluded my narrative, and may God persuade your hearts with His divine will and guidance in this matter."

Jezreel was tired and exhausted from many days of sharing his heart. So many things had happened since they arrived at the Temple. They had lost their home, and their dear friend Shekina. Little Mishi, it seemed, had grown in spirit and maturity. So often in those long days of waiting he had learned to pray for his dear Abba, and often he would speak to himself about the need to be strong and grow into a man like Jezreel. *"Mishi you must be strong for your Abba,"* he persuaded himself.

If Mishi could have had his way, he would have marched right into that chamber and told the priest they better cast the lot in favor of the scroll! But of course his growing maturity would not have permitted it. Besides, little Mishi had come to understand a divine truth: that it was better to leave everything in the hands of God's sovereignty.

After Jezreel had finished his address, Malchiah the High Priest gave instructions about the procedure they would follow in determining the scroll's validity. Each priest would be allowed to stand and give an argument concerning his own judgment, before the lot was cast. Jezreel was granted permission to remain in the chamber to hear their conclusions, and for this he was glad.

One by one each priest spoke. Some walked about the room venting their disapproval, as the sound of their voices echoed off the walls of the chamber. Words from those who proclaimed God's love too high and lofty a thing for a woman such as Gomer, stung at Jezreel's heart. Others walked over to him as they passionately spoke in favor of his testimony, and of the scrolls validity. As each priest concluded his own dissertation, it became apparent the priests were divided in their conclusions about the scroll. Three of them had spoken in favor of his father's writings, and three of them against.

Jezreel's eyes searched the room, for he knew that only one priest remained. Hachmoni would be the final voice to be heard, and then Malchiah would cast the lot, inviting the divine providence of God.

All the priests turned their attention to Hachmoni as they waited for him to begin his address. He walked into the center of the room, facing Jezreel. Hachmoni looked at him, as a man would look upon his dearest son. The good priest's hands were trembling slightly, as his fingers thoughtfully scratched at his beard. There had always been something about him, something that brought warmth to Jezreel's spirit. Even now, he was glad it was Hachmoni who would give the final address. From the second day when Hachmoni had brought Jezreel into this very chamber and exchanged greetings with him, Jezreel had known Hachmoni could be trusted. Now his father and mother's reputation, and the scrolls future, lay in Hachmoni's hands.

"I have served God faithfully for many years," he began, "and I have always found the providence of God to be an amazing thing. God, in His great wisdom, saw this day before it was ever lived. I am thankful to serve Him in this hour, and for this purpose. I too have heard all the address of Jezreel, concerning his father Hosea, and Gomer his mother. I have listened carefully both with my mind and my heart. I could have never imagined that I would serve God in such an important matter as this. But

God in His foreknowledge has so graciously placed me in His divine will. My brethren, I can assure you the things Jezreel has spoken are true."

Upon having said this, Hachmoni carefully positioned himself right next to where Jezreel was sitting. To everyone in the room this movement announced certain solidarity with Jezreel, an undeniable union. But when Hachmoni laid his hand on Jezreel's shoulder and started to speak again, everyone realized there was a bond between them that even Jezreel could never have imagined.

"I was a personal witness to the life of Hosea and Gomer," Hachmoni began once more. "I know Hosea's love for her was of divine nature. I know it was God who called him, and bid him to take Gomer to be his wife. For I served as a witness to all these things of which Jezreel has spoken, and, I am persuaded that God has brought us to this hour with a divine purpose; that the Word of God might be known."

No one in the room moved, as Jezreel squinted in deep thought. *"What could Hachmoni be talking about,"* he pondered?"

"Jezreel, I have something to tell you," Hachmoni said, looking right into his eyes. "You see, as you spoke you talked of a friend that lived by your father and mother, a friend who cared deeply for your father". Hachmoni looked around to all who were present, knowing that his next words would take everyone by surprise. "I am that friend you spoke of. I am he who lived by your father and mother all those many years. It was I on the roof with Hosea the night you were born. It was I

your father stayed with many nights, while he allowed
Gomer to abide in his own house. You were too young to
remember me before I left their community and came here
to the Temple to serve as a priest. But surely your father
has been faithful in committing to you the story of God's
will for his life. You see I came here to serve in the Temple
but a few weeks a year, and then, when I departed on the
day of which you spoke, I came here to live and serve,
giving myself wholly unto the Lord."

Jezreel was astonished. He leaned softly into
Hachmoni's arms, and embraced him as both men were
overcome with emotion. Hachmoni gently separated
them, by placing his hands on Jezreel's shoulders. "There
is much more to tell you my son," he said. "Your father and
I talked many hours about His call to take Gomer to be
his wife, and I know of a surety he loved her with all his
heart."

Hachmoni looked around the room once more,
now speaking to the other priests as well. "Hosea's love
for Gomer is an example to every one of us of God's divine
love for all mankind." He turned his attention again to
Jezreel, speaking tenderly to him. "I did not know what
had become of you Jezreel, or how to find you, until the
hour the scroll was discovered. Then I knew you must be
found, and given the opportunity to share your father's
story."

Jezreel could not believe his ears, and his mind was
racing so fast, filled with more questions than his mouth
could speak. Finally he broke, "do you know anything of
what may have become of my father and mother? Since

the day my dear Abba delivered me to Joanna, I only have heard rumors. Some have said a terrible thing befell them, others only kept silence, but my heart is so empty without knowing."

Hachmoni spoke again, "Yes my son, I know all that has befallen them. But I must tell you, it will grieve your very soul." Jezreel never flinched, for in his heart he had to know. "Say on, do not withhold from me a single word, for my heart aches to understand," he said.

Hachmoni smiled softly, knowing that all he would share would both heal, and sadden the heart of Jezreel. "My son, after you were sent away to live with Joanna, the anger and hatred from those in the community only grew worse. They despised your mother simply for her past, and for the pain she had inflicted upon your father. It was a good thing your father sent you away, lest harm would have befallen you."

Hachmoni began to walk around the room, perhaps to give his soul some release. "I was given leave by the priesthood for a short time to rest and take Sabbath. I returned to my home beside your father and mother and our friendship once again was established. One evening your father and mother, along with the good man Ishtob and I were taking bread on the rooftop of your parent's home. While there, some of the people from the community gathered below demanding that your father hand over Gomer to them. Their intention was to stone her to death.

But of course your father would never have done that! We all watched as Hosea went over and positioned himself on the edge of the roof. He began to shout down to them. He told them how much he loved Gomer. He told them of his forgiveness for her, and he bid the people to do the same."

Hachmoni stopped speaking, and lowered his head, because of the grief in sharing what would come next.

"As your father stood defending the cause of your mother, without warning an arrow was fired from the assembled crowd. It struck your father in the chest, piercing deep into his heart. He slowly buckled to his knees and fell to the roof. We expected the crowd to rush upon all of us, but instead, for some strange reason, they dispersed, leaving us to our sorrow. We all knelt over Hosea and found that he was still alive. As he gasped for his last remaining breaths he told us how much he loved us all. He told your mother that giving his life for her was worth all the joy her freedom had brought to him. Your mother was heartbroken as she stroked his face and wept. She believed that the arrow was meant for her, and that she was the one who deserved to die. Then your father began to speak of you Jezreel, how much he loved you. I watched as he slowly removed his signet seal from around his neck, and with his weak and trembling hands, he gave it to me. Your father begged me to one day find you, and present the seal to you, as a token of his love for you. That is why I gave it to you on the second day you came to the Temple to share with us the story of your father. After your father handed me the seal he slowly closed his eyes and passed. The next morning Ishtob and I took your father and buried him, and for both of us that was the saddest day of our lives. Soon thereafter Ishtob and I arranged for your mother to live out the remainder of her days in safety, down in the South Country. And there she died, I suppose of a broken heart. But she never grew weary talking about her love for Hosea, and the wonderful grace he had shown her."

Hachmoni then pulled from under his garment a document. "This Jezreel, is a last will and testament. I found it in some of Hosea's belongings after your mother had left. Your father's home was to be given to you. It is stated here in this deed that you were to inherit it. There is but one thing missing from the document that would make the inheritance yours. Your father died before he signed the document." Hachmoni laid the deed on the floor in front of Jezreel. "But you, my son, have the means to make it yours. All it needs is his signature," he said, with a wink.

Jezreel carefully removed the signet seal from his pocket and looked over to Malchiah, as if to gain his approval. Malchiah smiled broadly, and Jezreel gently placed the seal into a vessel of red Canaan dye provided by Hachmoni. He firmly pressed it onto the deed, leaving the name of Hosea clearly visible.

"Now your family has a home," Hachmoni said. You have a place where Mishi can live and become the godly man he longs to be.

Hachmoni turned to Malchiah. "My lord, it is my firm belief that this scroll should be included as sacred and holy, nothing less than the very Word of God; this is how I plea!"

Malchiah stood, carefully removing the Urim and the Thummin from the breast plate used at the Temple for casting lots. He held the two small disks tight in his hand as he spoke. "May the God of heaven direct us this day, in determining whether the scroll of Hosea should be honored as Thy Holy Word!" Then Malchiah cast the two disks on the table as all looked on. The disk rolled around and around, wobbling, until they both fell to the white side, the side that was counted as holy unto the Lord.

Elation filled the room!

"God has shown His perfect will," the High Priest said. "Let it be known today and throughout the Land Of Israel that God hath spoken through His mighty prophet Hosea! Let this scroll be regarded as Holy, and may it show forth God's love to all mankind throughout every generation!"

The End!

Cast of Characters & Meaning of Names

Hosea – "Salvation & Deliverer"

Gomer – "Complete"

Shekina – "Divine Glory"

Mishi– The fictional son of Jezreel and Anna

Jezreel– "God sows"

Anna – The fictional wife of Jezreel, "Grace"

King Hezekiah – "Jehovah is my strength"

Hachmoni – "Wise"

Ebed-Melech – "Servant of the king"

Zadok – "Righteous"

Malchiah – "My king is Jehovah"

Ira – "Watchful of a city"

Ishtob – "Man of Tob"

Diblaim – "Figs, and Fig Cakes"

Naomi – "My Delight"

Raphael – "God has healed"

Sennacherib – "Sin multiplied"

Isaiah – "Jehovah has saved"

Gabriella – "Strong through God"

Balak – "Devastator"

Serah – "The princess breathed"

Tryphon – "Delicacy"

Melea – "My dear friend: object of care"

Achaz – "Possessor"

Joanna – "Grace or gift of God"

Erelah – "Holy messenger" or "Angel"

About the Author

Terry Barnwell and his wife Sharon live in Knoxville, TN. He has been in ministry as a pastor for over thirty years in the Church of God of Prophecy.

He has long harbored a fascination with the Middle East and has spent many years researching the region and its biblical history. He regularly leads tours to Israel.

He is the founder of the Ancient Worlds Biblical Museum and Resource Center, an online community dedicated to biblical culture, archeology, and the country of Israel.

He is also the author of "Hosea: A Portrait of God's Love," a small group study published by White Wing Publishing House.

Pastor Barnwell is available for speaking engagements and may be contacted at ancientworldsmuseum@gmail.com.